CHINESE CELADON WARES

The Faber Monographs on Pottery and Porcelain
Edited by W. B. HONEY and ARTHUR LANE

★

A. *Northern Celadon. Bowl with carved peony decoration.*
Sung dynasty. Diameter 9½ in.
Capt. Dugald Malcolm. See pages 38–9

CHINESE CELADON WARES

by

G. St. G. M. GOMPERTZ

PITMAN PUBLISHING CORPORATION
NEW YORK

Printed it Great Britain

To
FUJIO KOYAMA
Whose keenness and integrity
set an example
to all students of Chinese ceramics

CONTENTS

ILLUSTRATIONS

COLOUR PLATES

MONOCHROME PLATES
after page 72

PREFACE

The writer of this short study of Chinese celadon has long felt that there is need to collate divergent Western and Oriental views on Chinese pottery and porcelain, not necessarily with the object of arriving at final conclusions, for these must often still be regarded as premature, but as a means of increasing our small fund of knowledge and stimulating further interest. Indeed, until fresh material becomes available as a result of new excavations in China, continued study must perforce largely consist in re-appraisal, and it is clearly desirable that this be made as comprehensive as possible. Since Japanese scholars have played a predominant part in Far Eastern research during the past thirty or more years, it is necessary to pay close attention to their work, which has been ably summarized in the writings of Fujio Koyama. It seems likely, however, that the main impetus in the future will come from the Chinese themselves. Indications of this trend are to be seen in many recent Chinese publications, among which special mention should be made of the brief historical survey of celadon wares by a scholar of long standing, Dr. Wan-li Chên, which was issued in Peking early last year.

Perhaps there is no province of Chinese ceramics in which Japanese views require more careful consideration than that of celadon. For this is a class of wares in which the Japanese have taken great aesthetic pleasure from the time it first became known to them in the eighth or ninth century, and their appreciation has been sharpened by long tradition and systematic training in the Tea Ceremony. Furthermore, their conceptions are sometimes at variance with those generally accepted in the West, and the reasons for such disagreement are not clearly understood. Western appraisal of Japanese studies has been impeded by the obstacles of an Oriental language and cast of thought, and there has been a similar failure on the part of Japanese scholars to grasp the critical and pragmatic methods of the West. Some progress can result from an exchange of views, and the prerequisite for this is a simple statement of the different opinions held together with the reasons or evidence on which they are based.

In view of the prevailing lack of information concerning Japanese research, it has been thought useful to include translations of relevant passages from Japanese sources, especially where these relate to actual field studies in China. Persistent efforts have been made by Japanese scholars to secure reliable data from the sites of ancient kilns, for it is on this in the final analysis that the identification of early wares must be based, and very little of their work has been published outside Japan. They have also had the advantage of readier access to the literature as well as to the places where the pottery was made. We should be the losers if we disregarded their views, but it would be equally misguided to accept their conclusions uncritically. The very fact that there continue to be different opinions will indicate the tentative nature of the study, for many problems must remain unsolved until further evidence is obtained and obscure records clarified.

The prime objective of this book is thus to provide a synthesis of views on the principal celadon wares and to illustrate these by a selection of representative examples drawn from collections in England and elsewhere.[1] Since celadon was widely made at provincial kilns all over China as well as at the main centres, it has been necessary to omit many types which are known only from literary references or have not yet been identified and fall outside the main groups. Several plates are included to show points of detail, especially the under-side and the foot, for the latter has been rightly termed the potter's 'signature' and provides the clearest indication of date, provenance and quality. The nature of the porcelain body also is apparent as a rule at the foot, and technical points such as the type of supports used in the kiln and the methods employed in cutting and shaping as well as in applying the glaze all stand revealed when a vessel is turned over and the underside examined.

Thanks are due to the museums and collectors who have generously facilitated the photography of specimens and permitted reproduction in this book, to Mr. Junkichi Mayuyama for assistance in procuring illustrations of pieces in Japan and to the proprietors of *Oriental Art* for allowing the republication in expanded form of material contributed to their journal on Yüeh ware. The author would like also to acknowledge his indebtedness to Sir Harry Garner and to Mr. Arthur Lane for helpful advice and suggestions.

G. St. G. M. G.
December 1957

[1] Eighty-three of the items illustrated are in public or private collections in England, thirty-one are in Japan and eleven in the U.S.A.

CHINESE DYNASTIES
AND PERIODS

SHANG-YIN		1766–1122 B.C.
CHOU		1122– 249 B.C.
Warring States	481– 221 B.C.	
CH'IN		221– 206 B.C.
HAN		206 B.C.–A.D. 220
SIX DYNASTIES		220– 589
SUI		581– 618
T'ANG		618– 906
FIVE DYNASTIES		907– 960
Wu-Yüeh	907– 978	
SUNG		960–1279
Northern Sung	960–1127	
Southern Sung	1127–1279	
YÜAN		1280–1368
MING		1368–1643
CH'ING		1644–1912

INTRODUCTION

Among early Chinese ceramic wares none have achieved greater fame or been admired more widely than the celadons. The name celadon is believed to have been taken from that of a character in a French seventeenth-century play who always appeared on the stage dressed in grey-green clothing.[1] Like other equally vague terms, it has come into general use among students of ceramics and is considered a suitable, if imprecise, description for a wide range of Chinese and other porcelains. It may be regarded as the equivalent of the Chinese *ch'ing tz'u* and the Japanese *seiji*, both meaning green (or blue) porcelain, but there has been a conventional limitation in its use in the West to such wares as Lung-ch'üan, 'Northern Celadon' and Yüeh. There is no reason why it should not also be used of some other wares which the Chinese literature describes as *ch'ing*, sometimes with a qualifying prefix such as *fên* (pale or soft), signifying many different or variable shades of blue and green. This is the current practice both in China and Japan, where Ju and Kuan are regarded as celadon no less than the wares to which the term has been commonly applied in the West.

In order to make the position clear, it will be advisable to start with an acceptable definition of celadon and then specify certain types which are considered to fall outside the bounds of our survey. Celadon may be held strictly to denote high-fired porcellanous wares with a felspathic glaze of characteristic bluish or greyish green tone derived from iron. From a technical standpoint there is ground for including Chün ware among the celadons, for the colour of the glaze is now known to be attributable to iron and it is, of course, described as *ch'ing* in the Chinese literature. However, it is difficult to associate the intense blue of most Chün wares with the term celadon, and only passing reference will here be made to Chün in discussing various kinds of northern wares. A somewhat analogous case is that of celadons which have turned light grey or brown as a result of oxidation in the firing.[2] Although the in-

---

[1] The shepherd Céladon in one of the plays founded on the romance, *L'Astrée*, written by Honoré d'Urfé.

[2] There are many fine examples of this type, especially among Southern Kuan ware; most of these were formerly regarded as *Ko* ware by reason of their profuse crackle. It is an open question whether the colour, known to the Chinese as *mi sê*, or the light brown of roasted rice, was produced deliberately or not. The fact that it is

gredients are the same, the result is entirely different, and here also it has seemed that colour should be the guide; this compels us to omit from our illustrations some beautiful specimens which do not fully satisfy the requirements of the term, equivocal as it may be.

Long before celadon became known in Europe it was held in high esteem throughout the Orient. Yüeh ware was exported to India, Persia and Egypt in the T'ang period and after. Lung-ch'üan celadon became so famous during the Sung and Ming periods that exports from China reached staggering proportions. Thousands of celadon fragments have been picked up on the beach at Kamakura, the contemporary capital of Japan, while at the opposite extremity of Asia an incredible number of celadons were collected by the Sultans of Turkey, some thirteen hundred of which are still kept at the Topkapu Palace in Istanbul. The mysterious beauty of the celadon glaze gave rise to various fables: in Japan legendary properties were ascribed to famous specimens of the ware and in the Near East and Europe it was believed that celadon dishes would disclose the presence of poison in food.

One of the earliest pieces of celadon to arrive in this country probably was the celebrated 'Warham bowl', owned by New College, Oxford, though there appears to be no proof that it was bequeathed by Archbishop Warham in 1530, as often supposed. Many other celadons in English collections are said to have come from India, Persia and Egypt. In recent years the greater proportion has been obtained from China itself, many of the Sung pieces being wasters, or discards, found at the kiln sites; but some of the finest celadons in the David Foundation were acquired in Japan.

The beauty and subtlety of the various types of celadon glaze, ranging from light green through bluish green to olive or dove-grey, have been explained scientifically by research into the chemistry of these effects. Primarily they are all due to iron, chiefly in the ferrous condition, but the resulting tone has also depended on a number of other factors, such as the composition of the paste and glaze, the temperature at which firing took place, the atmospheric conditions inside the kiln during the firing and the presence of unfused particles and minute bubbles, which are held in suspension in the glaze and exert a scattering effect on light. The result has been to give celadon wares a great variety of shade and texture with a translucence which ranges from a gem-like lustre to a subdued sheen. Their beauty is essentially of a sensuous order and can best be appreciated by handling as well as observing specimens. A jade-like quality was particularly admired by the

so uniform, as well as having a mellow charm of its own, indicates that it is unlikely to have been the result of faulty technique, and it is generally assumed to have been contrived on account of its special appeal.

Chinese and must often have been the objective, for jade was prized above all other stones and regarded as the most precious material in existence.

Iron oxide must be fired in a reducing atmosphere to produce ferrous iron, from which the loveliest celadons derive their colour, and Koyama has laid great stress on the significance of wood-fuel, which he believes was largely used in the kilns of central and southern China and resulted in the great development of celadon wares in that region. In the north coal was used more generally, with the result that the glaze tended to become oxidized—hence the olive-green or brownish tone often assumed by Northern Celadon. Like all generalizations, however, this view should not be pressed too far: fine, jade-like celadons were produced in the north as well as in the south, and the astonishing thing is that the Chinese potter, by empirical means, was able to maintain such mastery over the production of high-fired porcelain.[1] As Koyama remarks: 'It was no easy task two thousand years ago to raise the temperature of ceramic wares to such a high point; it seems to me that this could only have been accomplished as a result of the illimitable perseverance which has been a racial characteristic of the Chinese from early times.'

With increased knowledge and equipment the modern potter has been able to make celadons which are technically flawless yet lack some indefinable quality pervading the early Chinese wares. Expert craftsmen have in rare cases succeeded in making such close copies of Lung-ch'üan celadon as to deceive the most experienced; however, their achievement is less remarkable when we recall that Lung-ch'üan, like most of the early wares, was mass-produced, and the great majority of the specimens which excite so much admiration were thus standardized rather than individual productions.

Among Chinese celadons the Sung wares must on all counts be ranked supreme. The early Yüeh *pi-sê* ware, much praised by poets and regarded as a peak of porcelain manufacture, has not been identified with certainty and may not have survived, while virtually nothing is known about the contemporary Ch'ai ware, literary references to which border on the mythical. But we have abundant evidence that Ju and other northern wares, together with the Kuan ware of Hangchou and the many varieties of celadon made around Lung-ch'üan in

---

[1] In the West celadon is normally regarded as porcellanous stoneware rather than true porcelain, the essential characteristics of which are considered to be whiteness and translucence; however, we shall henceforth use the term porcelain in the broad Far Eastern sense, signifying hardness and resonance, and apply it indiscriminately to the celadon wares. For an interesting study of this question the reader is referred to Gustaf Lindberg's 'Porcellanous Ware—Porcelain: Remarks concerning some early ceramic wares of China,' *Ethnos*, No. 4, 1947, pp. 95–105.

the south, attained an excellence of glaze and style which has never been surpassed. The beauty and character of these wares may in some degree derive from the very conditions of uncertainty and technical limitation under which the potters worked. Intuitive skill in matching means to material was no doubt a vital factor in their achievement; happy chances sometimes played a part, and imperfections became irrelevant or even contributed toward the total effect.

1

THE ORIGIN OF CELADON

Very little is known about the beginnings of stoneware, or high-fired pottery, and the introduction of felspathic glazes. The tendency of modern research is constantly to set back to an earlier period developments which had been accepted as occurring at a particular time, and the farther such events recede into the past, the more difficult it becomes to determine their cause and sequence. Most of our present knowledge rests on chance discoveries and the results of uncontrolled excavations; the available evidence, therefore, is insufficient to allow more than an indication of the probable trend as a basis for further research.

Felspathic material requires a fluxing agent, such as potash obtained from wood-ash, in order to make it fuse readily, and it seems likely that glazing in the first place came about by accident, as a result of wood-ash from the faggots used in firing the kiln falling on the heated pottery. There are many examples of early Chinese and Korean stoneware which show a glaze-like effect, especially round the shoulders of jars and vases, caused by this entirely natural process. In the West this is known as 'kiln gloss', but the more appropriate term used in Japan is 'natural glaze' (*shizen-yu*). In some cases this fortuitous glaze is so thick and lustrous that it cannot easily be differentiated from the deliberate glazing which must have come into use very shortly afterwards.

It would seem that artificial glaze material was next introduced into the kiln or applied to vessels in such a way as to accentuate the natural process just described and to produce a more even and consistent effect. It is found mainly on the upper parts of vessels, often running down in thick drops or waves toward the base, and we may surmise that at this stage the potters were content to increase the supply of ash or other material and allow matters to take their natural course. The Western tendency to regard such effects as deliberate and controlled does not seem fully warranted, for it ignores the fact that glaze is rarely found on parts protected from falling ashes, such as beneath the mouth and round the neck. On the other hand, the Japanese view that they are

1

entirely accidental seems questionable for the reason that the glaze is often remarkably dense and even, or is roughly demarcated by incised lines and patterns. Some combination of natural and artificial methods would seem to correspond more closely with the facts as observed.

Later it is evident that improved means were adopted, such as applying glaze with a brush or dipping the vessels into it so that the entire surface could be covered. This made it necessary to raise the vessels on stilts or spurs, for otherwise their flat bases would become fused to the supporting stands, and the next step was to eliminate or at least reduce the marks left by the spurs. Sometimes this was effected by firing vessels in the reverse position, standing on their mouth-rims, and then fixing a metal covering to the unglazed rims.

The origin of celadon is likewise a problem which remains to be unravelled. It is quite possible that the most primitive celadons will finally be traced back to a time not far removed from the earliest use of an artificial glaze, but here also the material available for study is far too scanty to enable any definite conclusions to be reached. The achievement of a reducing atmosphere inside the kiln may originally have been the result of chance, like the production of the glaze itself. Increased efficiency in the construction of kilns and use of wood-fuel for stoking the fires probably brought about improvements in the tone and quality of the glaze. Persistent efforts no doubt were made to utilize superior and more highly refined material and to establish complete mastery over the firing conditions.

Thus, the earliest examples of wares with a celadon or 'pre-celadon' glaze commonly exhibit a brownish or olive-coloured tone resulting from imperfect firing conditions and consequent oxidation. Later specimens show an improvement in the glaze colour, which is often pale green, though still sometimes tinged with olive. The peak of perfection is attained by the bluish green glazes of the Kuan, Ju and Lung-ch'üan wares dating from the Sung period, while the 'sea-green' glaze of Yüan and early Ming celadon is often hardly less accomplished.

Some further explanation of the terms oxidation and reduction may be desirable at this point. All celadon wares owe their colour to the presence of a small amount of iron, usually from one to three per cent; the yellower tones are given by ferric oxide and the bluer by ferrous oxide. The glaze normally contains a high percentage of feldspar and a smaller amount of silica; its quality depends to a large extent on the character of the silica and the care given to grinding the material. However, perhaps nothing is so important as the firing: where this is carried out in such a way that combustion is complete and there is an ample supply of oxygen, the metallic constituents of the clay and glaze produce their oxide colours, but where combustion is incomplete or smoky, the carbon present seizes as much of the available oxygen as possible, reducing the iron oxide to a ferrous state. In simpler language, iron has the characteristic of becoming bluish when reduced and brown or yellow when oxidized. Consequently, where a celadon is bluish green, it has been produced by a reducing atmosphere, and where it has turned brown, some degree of oxidation has taken place and it is said to be oxidized. In theory a neutral atmosphere lies half-way between these two extremes, but in practice this usually results in some unevenness or variation in the tone.

Many primitive celadon wares have been recovered from old graves in all parts of China. The greatest number has been found in Chekiang province in the region of Hangchou, but recent excavations carried out by the Chinese authorities have brought to light numerous examples dating from the Han and Six Dynasties periods both north of the Yangtze and far to the west. Some of the earliest pieces, including several examples in the Ingram Collection, are believed to have come from Shao-hsing, the former capital of the state of Yüeh, and have been tentatively assigned to the third century B.C. by reason of their close resemblance to late Chou ritual bronzes.[1] They have been described as predecessors of the famous Yüeh ware made several centuries later in the same district. Although there has been some disagreement on the subject of dating, there can be little doubt that these specimens are among the most archaic of Chinese porcellanous wares (1). They are characterized by somewhat crude, bronze-like forms, a vitreous, olive-coloured glaze and impressed or stamped decoration of spirals and rope-bands. They seem to be clearly recognizable as precursors of the late Han and Six Dynasties Yüeh ware, and it may be assumed that they represent the ancestral type from which Yüeh ware was developed; but further study and additional evidence are necessary to enable their sequence and dating to be convincingly demonstrated.

[1] Orvar Karlbeck, 'Early Yüeh Ware,' *Oriental Art* (Old Series), Vol. 2, No. 1, Summer 1949; also: Walter Hochstadter, 'Pottery and Stonewares of Shang, Chou and Han,' *Bulletin of the Museum of Far Eastern Antiquities*, No. 24, 1952, p. 100.

(1) *Plates 1 and 2.*

2

YÜEH WARE

In the opening chapters of this book stress has been laid on the fame and beauty of Chinese celadon; it remains to add a few words concerning its importance in the history of Chinese pottery and porcelain. For this has only become apparent during the past twenty or thirty years and is perhaps not sufficiently realized even now. Baron Ozaki, for many years a leading Japanese authority, has stated: 'Celadons are the most important of all early Chinese ceramic wares and their study forms the very basis for research into early Chinese ceramics.' Koyama recently described celadon as the 'backbone' of Oriental ceramics and has devoted his only full-length work on ceramics to the history of Chinese celadon wares. It is significant that nearly half this important study is taken up by a comprehensive survey of Yüeh ware.

By general consent the term Yüeh has nowadays been extended to cover most, if not all, the early celadon wares manufactured in Chekiang province, in the general area of Hangchou, as well as the later *pi-sê yao* of Chinese literary fame, which became the special ware reserved for use by the Ruling House of the State of Wu-Yüeh. Whereas the Sung celadons reached their zenith and endured for less than three centuries, Yüeh ware developed slowly over a period of about one thousand years, from the Han dynasty to the early Sung. It is the measure of our ignorance of early Chinese pottery that Yüeh ware was only identified in the early 'thirties, after Dr. Nakao had sent to the British Museum shards collected at the newly discovered site at Shang-lin-hu in Yü-yao hsien. Recent archaeological investigations in China have underlined the significance of Yüeh ware; a vast amount of material is now being accumulated, and we may hope that this will throw further light on such obscure matters as the transition from stoneware to true porcelain.

There is no more romantic ware than Yüeh. Poets of the T'ang period vied with each other in praising the mystery and beauty of 'the porcelain of Yüeh-chou'. The following lines are taken from the verses of Lu Kuei-mêng, a poet of the ninth century (Bushell's translation):

4

'The misty scenery of late autumn appears when the Yüeh kilns
    are thrown open:
'The thousand peaks have been despoiled of their bright colour for
    the decoration of the bowls.
'Let us take them out at midnight to collect the falling dew,
'Or fill up the cups with wine in emulation of Chi Chung-san.'

Another celebrated verse composed by the T'ang poet Hsü Yin refers to
a service of *pi-sê* tea-bowls made for presentation to the Emperor
(again using Bushell's translation):

'Like bright moons cunningly carved and dyed with spring water:
Like curling disks of thinnest ice, filled with green clouds:
Like ancient moss-eaten bronze mirrors lying upon the mat:
Like tender lotus leaves full of dewdrops floating on the river-side.'

Some *pi-sê* wares were sent as gifts by neighbouring rulers; thus Prince
Wang of Shu sent to Chu, Prince of Liang, gold-rimmed bowls, of
which it was said (here we use Bushell's translation as amended by Sir
Percival David):

'The gold rims protect the glaze of the precious bowls;
The secret colour brings out the tone of the blue-green ware.'

Yüeh tea-bowls were considered preferable to all others. The famous
'Tea Classic' of the T'ang writer Lu Yü rates them more highly than
the silvery-white wares of Hsing-chou. Various reasons were given for
this preference: the colour resembled ice or jade and was thus considered superior to any other, or it was thought to enhance the beauty
of the tea by deepening its green tone instead of changing this to red
or black.

All these descriptions relate to the Yüeh ware of the ninth or tenth
century, the period when it grew famous throughout the Orient under
the name of *pi-sê*. Sir Percival David has shown that there is good
reason for supposing that this name underwent a change of meaning.
At first it meant 'secret colour', referring to the mysterious beauty of
the glaze, but later it was applied to the products of the same Yüeh-
chou factory after these had been reserved exclusively for use by the
Ruling House of Wu-Yüeh; thus it came to be used in the secondary
sense of 'prohibited colour', and the original meaning either lapsed or
was forgotten.[1] This, however, was the culminating point in the long
history of Yüeh ware, and it is necessary to return to the early period
when Yüeh celadon first emerged.

[1] Sir Percival David, 'Some Notes on Pi-sê Yao,' *Eastern Art*, Vol. I, January
1929, p. 139.

We have seen that the most primitive wares of celadon type are thought to date from the third century B.C., or the period of the War-ring States, and seem to represent the forerunners of Yüeh ware. This strengthens the view that Yüeh ware originated in some part of the Han period immediately following. After his investigation of the Yüeh kilns at Chiu-yen, Brankston showed in a brief but convincing article that there were numerous Han-style Yüeh wares, many of which were probably made at Chiu-yen, and that the period during which the Chiu-yen kilns were active could be reliably placed at the first to the sixth century of our era.[1] In the course of his argument Brankston referred briefly to several jars in the Historical Museum at Peking which had been excavated from a tomb dated the eleventh year of Yung-yüan in the Han dynasty, or A.D. 99. Karlbeck and Hoch-stadter give further particulars of these important relics, which in-cluded basins decorated with diamond diaper bands and are known as the Hsinyang pottery from their place of discovery in southern Honan.[2]

The excavations at Hsinyang were carried out early in 1924 by the late Carl Whiting Bishop on behalf of the Chinese Government, and Karlbeck quotes an interesting letter he received from Bishop shortly after the work was completed. This states that the brick bearing a *nien hao* corresponding to the year A.D. 99, though not coming from either of the two graves excavated, was found in the area between them and was of precisely the same type as those used for constructing the tombs, while coins found in both tombs indicated a similar date. The view that the celadons came from a Han tomb has been endorsed also by such noted Chinese and Japanese scholars as Dr. Wan-li Chên and Dr. Sueji Umehara. Bishop goes on to relate the astonishment felt by the excavators at finding what they at first took to be Sung celadons in a Han grave; but, after cleaning the pottery, they saw that it was 'an ancestral form of celadon . . . more than pottery but not quite porce-lain'. Koyama, who was able to examine the Hsinyang relics during a visit to Peking, describes the wares as follows:

'The glaze and style are similar and the wares seem to have been made at the same time and probably in the same kiln. The body material is light grey and hard, fine-grained, semi-porcellanous. The glaze is semi-transparent and light olive in colour; however, parts that are mis-fired are opaque and sometimes have a rough surface. Some

[1] A. D. Brankston, 'Yüeh Ware of the "Nine Rocks" Kiln,' *The Burlington Magazine*, Vol. LXXIII, December 1938.

[2] Orvar Karlbeck, 'Proto-Porcelain and Yüeh Ware,' *O.C.S. Transactions*, Vol. 25, 1949–50; Walter Hochstadter, 'Pottery and Stonewares of Shang, Chou and Han,' *Bulletin of the Museum of Far Eastern Antiquities*, No. 24, 1952, p. 100. For illustrations of the Hsinyang finds, see the author's 'Some Notes on Yüeh Ware,' *Oriental Art*, (New Series) Vol. II, No. 1, Spring 1956.

have crazing over the entire surface, and some have stamped network decoration.'

This description agrees very well with others published, except that Bishop terms the glaze 'a pale greenish hue, recalling that on some early Korean pottery' and Hochstadter refers to the 'grey-green to sea-green tone'. All authorities stress the similarity of the Hsinyang pottery to Yüeh ware of the Six Dynasties period, and Koyama believes that the Hsinyang celadons were actually made at Tê-ch'ing, the ealiest known Yüeh kiln centre. The significance of the discovery is that it establishes beyond reasonable doubt the origin of Yüeh ware in the Han period, as maintained by Brankston. This is a matter of importance because no conclusive argument can be based on stylistic evidence alone for the reason that Han forms and decoration evidently continued well into the subsequent Six Dynasties era.

Although no other Yüeh specimens have yet been recovered from dated Han tombs, there are numerous examples made in characteristic Han style and the more primitive of these may be reasonably assigned to the Han period (1). They include large basins and dishes with flat bases corresponding in form and decoration with dated Han bronzes (2), wine-cups similar to the lacquer wares recovered from Han sites (3), incense burners of the familiar 'hill-jar' shape and lamp-stands in the form of bears (4) or vessels with bear-legs. Han pottery wares of identical type are not uncommon but are either unglazed or covered with a low-temperature lead glaze, whereas the specimens just mentioned have been fired at a high temperature and exhibit a definite though primitive celadon glaze.

A number of Yüeh kiln sites have been located, but attention will here be confined to the three most important, at Tê-ch'ing, Chiu-yen and Shang-lin-hu, which were evidently the centres of extensive potteries.

TÊ-CH'ING

Tê-ch'ing is the earliest Yüeh kiln centre so far discovered and is located some twenty-five miles to the north of Hangchou; it was found in October 1930 by Mr. Tsuneo Yonaiyama, who was then Japanese consul at Hangchou. Owing to pressure of his official duties, Mr. Yonaiyama did not make his discovery known until 1939, when he published his book *Shina Fudoki* (Chinese Customs), from which the extracts given below are all taken. A few years after this the Tê-ch'ing shards were exhibited at the Nezu Museum in Tokyo, where they caused something of a sensation.

---

(1) *Plates* 3–6; (2) *Plate* 5; (3) *Plate* 4B; (4) *Plate* 6A.

Mr. Yonaiyama relates that his interest was first aroused by the place-name *Hou-yao*, because the Chinese word *yao* signifies 'ware' or 'kiln'. He decided to visit the locality and set out by boat along a winding canal from the town Tê-ch'ing: 'Slowly we approached a mountain. I was told that Hou-yao lay beyond it. A few farmhouses stood here and there in the mulberry plantation—it was a small hamlet in a little valley.' He proceeded to visit house after house, inquiring whether anyone knew of any pottery kilns, past or present, in the district. After many fruitless attempts, he at last found an old man who said he knew of a place where bowls were once made. Guided by this old man and in drizzling rain he approached the mountain by a narrow path and came to a place where the rice-fields merged into pine woods, which clothed the lower slopes of the mountain. Fragments of pottery were to be seen everywhere in the upturned soil of the rice-fields. The account is of sufficient interest to be quoted verbatim—though of course by translation:

'This is what the old man told me:—"Once upon a time bowls were made here. My father told me about it when I was a child. He said it was thousands of years ago. This is the only place where one can find pieces of pottery. They get in my way, so I throw them aside. They have gradually become fewer in number." Some other villagers had joined us and surrounded the old man, listening to his tale. Pointing to the scattered fragments of bowls, some with grey or grey-green glaze, others with black *temmoku* glaze, he continued:—"These greyish pieces come out in great numbers; there are black ones also, but they are scarce. Mostly they come from bowls—you don't find such things as pots or jars."

'The dozen or more peasants who had gathered round were all good-natured people. Seeing me listening so attentively to what the old man had to tell and collecting potsherds from the soil, they helped to find more. Some of them remarked that they had better pieces at home and went off to fetch them; they returned with bowls of various sizes, which they presented to me, saying that they had all been found in this place.

'I was unable to look for additional kiln sites in the vicinity because of the rain and the tall grass which covered the ground in the pine woods and up to the mountain. . . .'

On the way back to Tê-ch'ing Yonaiyama had the good fortune to discover another kiln site. He was lying relaxed in the boat as it passed through a narrow section of the canal, 'entirely preoccupied with the boat trip and the scenery', when he suddenly became aware of a layer of potsherds at about water level on both banks. Quickly landing, he found that the area was a mulberry plantation and the ground up to the foot of the mountain was littered with potsherds.

Yonaiyama collected a considerable number of shards at the two kiln sites, most of which were of the early celadon type. In addition, he gathered evidence of the kilns themselves in the form of saggars, pottery wares fused to their stands, several bowls fused together and partly melted bricks. There can be no doubt that these relics, which the writer was able to examine at Yonaiyama's home in Tokyo, represent one of the most important discoveries of their kind in recent years. Although it has been impossible for a thorough investigation of the area to be carried out, it is evident that a group of early kilns was established in the vicinity of Tê-ch'ing during the Han period and onward into the Six Dynasties. The wares made at this centre closely resemble those from Chiu-yen but seem to be somewhat earlier in type, as will appear from Koyama's brief description of the shards given below:

'The celadon shards are characterized by their grey-green glaze and have a hard, semi-porcellanous body with some iron content. In general they are modelled after Han bronzes and are large and strong with flat bases. For ewers, spouts shaped like chickens' heads were popular and angular ears are characteristic (1). The glaze is very like that of Chiu-yen wares, so that it is difficult to differentiate at first glance, but the Tê-ch'ing body is harder, crazing is less common and the glaze colour seems somewhat greener.'

Some of the shards had iron-brown spots or splashes as a form of decoration. The same ferric oxide spots are found on specimens believed to have been made at Chiu-yen, including several pieces in the Ingram Collection, and it is likely that this style was practised at several of the Yüeh potteries. Koyama also states that the Tê-ch'ing shards immediately reminded him of the Hsinyang pottery he had seen in Peking, some being almost identical in form, paste and glaze. He considers that the Tê-ch'ing kilns are of rare significance, since they may be presumed to date from the Han period, continuing thereafter into the Six Dynasties.

CHIU-YEN

Reference has already been made to Brankston's excellent article on his visit to the Chiu-yen kilns, some thirty miles to the south-east of Hangchou, in the summer of 1937. Unfortunately his report obscured the fact that the kiln site had already been investigated in July 1936 by Mr. Yuzō Matsumura, successor to Yonaiyama as Japanese consul at Hangchou. The credit for the discovery must therefore go to Matsumura, though it should be noted that the term 'discovery' is to be

(1) *Plate* 8B.

understood in the sense of 'investigating and making generally known', for the original discoverers in this case as in so many others were peasants, who sought to make a profit from their treasure-trove, and art-dealers, who hastened to explore the source of the articles brought to them. Thus, Matsumura states:

'It became known that a kiln site had recently been discovered at Chiu-yen in Shao-hsing hsien, and excavated articles had been brought to the Hangchou market. So, by taking advantage of the first Sunday in July, I was able to undertake an exploration trip to the Chiu-yen site, accompanied by an interpreter.

'We crossed the Ch'ien-tang river, hired a taxi and reached a village where we transferred to a small boat. The boat was long and narrow, with the top covered like those often seen in Chinese southern paintings. The boatman sat in the bows and pulled an oar with both hands, while working another with his feet.

'It was 9.20 a.m. when we left. The canal here is the large and well-known one leading from Hangchou, along which petrol-driven motor boats were running busily to and fro. We left the big canal on the outskirts of a small town and entered a river to the right, making for a range of mountains. It was a small river, only 30 ft. wide at the narrowest part and 60 ft. wide at the broadest, with a very sluggish flow of water. The land on either side was mostly paddy-fields, and the transplanting of the rice was almost all finished. Under the green trees were the water-wheels used for pumping water into the paddy-fields: these so-called "dragon-wheels" made a roaring noise as they turned.

'As the boatman was said to have taken Hangchou art-dealers to Chiu-yen on three previous occasions, he knew the place well and tied up the boat close to the location of the ancient kiln site. There were low hills about one mile west of the river, so that I was afraid I would have to walk over to them if the kilns were of the sloping type, and I felt loath to do this in the terrific heat. However, I was relieved to find that the kiln site was very close at hand—not more than fifty feet from the river bank. . . .

'It was covered with a bamboo grove and set at an inclination of between 15 and 25 degrees toward the south. Countless fragments of pottery and saggars were scattered in the area between the lowest part of the grove and the larger trees. It seemed that all the shards with fairly good decoration had already been taken, and those I saw were mostly from plain or flat bowls and had only a belt of diamond diaper pattern on the sides. However, their glaze was generally greener and more lustrous than that of fragments collected at Yü-yao on the shores of Lake Shang-lin. . . .'[1]

[1] Yuzō Matsumura, 'Exploration of Yüeh Kiln Sites,' (in Japanese), *Tōji*, Vol.

Matsumura's account of the specimens he collected on the site is also worth quoting:

'The largest number were from flat bowls, and these were followed by others from jars and flower-vases. The figurine mentioned earlier and two ink-pallets, which I collected myself, are rare pieces. These ink-pallets are of the type which does not have a depressed portion. The ink-stone is rubbed on their round, smooth, flat surface and there is a somewhat highly raised border all round to prevent the water from spilling. For decorative reasons there are four legs. An interesting point is that on these particular ink-pallets—unlike the other wares—the base was glazed, also the feet, but the part on which the ink-stone is rubbed was left bare. The ink was helped to flow by very fine marks of the potter's wheel, showing an *expertise* unusual for the time.

'Some of the flat bowls were plain, but most had simple decoration round the mouth. Eighty or ninety per cent of these were diamond diaper pattern, encircling the mouth of the bowl in a band about one inch wide (1). A thick line was drawn above or below this—or above *and* below it. The diamond diaper pattern is so well executed that it seems to have been stamped on to the bowls, but close examination shows that it was made with an implement like a chopstick, with a square point, and the glaze settled more thickly in the indentations, making these a deeper green, while the raised parts are white and form a design with white slanting lines. Simply as a result of skilled craftsmanship by hand, a beautiful pattern has come into being.[1]

'The more elaborately made bowls have decoration of chrysanthemums stamped in a row above or below the diamond diaper pattern (2); there is also a wave or wave and arabesque pattern, while some other pieces are specially elaborate and have lions' or chickens' heads in relief on the shoulders. These are simple but vigorous in appearance, conveying a strong impression like the works of a noted sculptor. There are also many specimens which have either two or

VIII, No. 5, October 1936. While Matsumura's investigations were conducted in great heat, Brankston in the following year had to contend with heavy rain. Matsumura evidently saw the actual site of one of the kilns, with its quantities of waste matter; Brankston was less fortunate, being taken to some fields and told that the pottery was several feet underground. He states specifically: 'There was nothing to see on the surface'. However, the villagers brought him numerous shards, which they were glad to sell, and a small boy raked the bed of the river with a hoe and 'fished up several wasters from under the water.' He concludes: 'So our kiln site was found,' for the evidence clearly showed that Chiu-yen had been an ancient kiln centre; but it seems unlikely that he ever saw the individual site in the bamboo grove to which Matsumura refers.

[1] This theory seems very questionable; in most cases the design was evidently produced by stamping.

(1) *Plates* 3A *and* B; (2) *Plates* 3A *and* 4B.

four simple "ears" instead of lions' heads. Compared with the Yü-yao (Shang-lin-hu) wares, both the incised and relief designs are more robust and masculine.

'In general the glaze colour is a clear olive-green, but sometimes it is brown. Some excavated Yü-yao wares have a beautiful green glaze like pine-needles, but others are a greyish olive colour and not to our taste; as regards the technique also, while some are delicate and refined, well suited for use by aristocrats, others are poorly made and seem better fitted for coolies. Thus, there is a wide diversity in the quality of Yü-yao wares, as with gems mixed among stones. But the Chiu-yen wares are all about the same quality and have uniform glaze colour and simple technique. Possibly the reason for this is that the Yü-yao kilns were in operation for a long period of time from the T'ang dynasty through the Five Dynasties to the Sung, whereas the Chiu-yen kilns were active for a shorter period from the middle of the T'ang to the Five Dynasties and show the strong impress of this era.

'Some of the Chiu-yen specimens are not at all inferior when compared with high-grade Yü-yao wares: for example, the large ewer with the chicken-head spout in my possession is quite up to the standard of Yü-yao wares in glaze colour, technique, etc.—in fact it rather surpasses them in archaic elegance. I am often tempted to question the accepted view that the Yüeh ware praised by the T'ang poet Lu Kuei-mêng in his celebrated verse came from Yü-yao and to believe that it is more likely to have been made at Chiu-yen.'

Commenting on this report of Matsumura's, Koyama asserts that it 'tells us everything about the Yüeh ware from Chiu-yen, failing to mention only the body'. As already noted, the body closely resembles that of Tê-ch'ing ware, being semi-porcellanous and with a rather large iron content. Koyama states that it 'gives a softer impression' than Tê-ch'ing ware, but this varies according to the conditions under which it was fired and sometimes it is impossible to distinguish between the two. According to Koyama, the glaze is often somewhat oxidized, so that Chiu-yen ware more frequently shows the putty colour associated with Yüeh yao, but 'well reduced specimens are very difficult to differentiate from Tê-ch'ing ware'. With regard to dating, Koyama disagrees with the view put forward by Matsumura, holding with Brankston that the period of activity lasted from late Han through the Six Dynasties, though he admits that positive evidence is still lacking.

It is perhaps unnecessary to quote from Western authorities or to describe such distinctive Chiu-yen features as the concave base and brown 'haloes', where the pieces rested on irregular lumps of clay, because these and others are already well known and publicized. Those

12

interested in pursuing the matter further may be referred to Karl-beck's very thorough survey based on the Ingram Collection, which contains the largest group of Chiu-yen and other Yüeh wares in exist-ence (p. 6, footnote 2). The Chiu-yen tendency to grotesquerie may, however, be noted: besides the bowls, jars and ewers with their animal masks or chicken-head spouts there are many bizarre animal forms, such as water-droppers in the shape of frogs or toads and light-stands or water-pots modelled out of lions, bears or monkeys (1).

Most of the examples of Chiu-yen ware so far recovered probably came from graves in the Shao-hsing district, a large number of which were excavated during construction of a new road early in 1936. Koyama states that the curio shops at Hangchou and Shanghai were subsequently 'flooded with the wares'. There had, of course, already been much grave-robbery in the same district, and the new finds led to further depredations, so that an estimated two or three thousand tombs were opened and pillaged. Many of these also contained bricks and bronze mirrors stamped with year-marks of the Six Dynasties period; similar evidence showed that a few were of later date—Sui, T'ang and Sung. The pottery comprised jars, dishes, bowls, basins, wine-cups, light-stands, ladles and various kinds of mortuary vessels. A considerable number of these articles found their way to Japan.

The Chiu-yen kilns were only a few miles from Shao-hsing, so there is good reason to suppose that most of the wares unearthed from graves in the locality were made at these kilns, especially as they present the same features and are of the same type as the shards and wasters found at Chiu-yen. However, some may have come from other Yüeh kilns in the vicinity. Koyama mentions a Yüeh kiln site discovered at Fu-yang hsien, further up the River Ch'ien-tang from Hangchou, and recent reports from China state that kiln sites have also been located at Shang-tung, about thirty miles south of Hangchou, and at Wang-chia-lü, a few miles south of Chiu-yen, where the products seem to have been almost identical to those made at Chiu-yen. Some charac-teristic examples of this type of Six Dynasties Yüeh ware are shown in our illustrations (2).

SHANG-LIN-HU

Although the early Yüeh kiln centres of Tê-ch'ing and Chiu-yen are of great importance in Chinese ceramic history, the kilns beside Lake Shang-lin in Yü-yao hsien attained far greater fame both in the T'ang period, when they seem to have reached a peak of activity, and

(1) *Plates* 6A *and* 7B; (2) *Plates* 3, 5, 6 *and* 7B.

in our own times, when their discovery resulted in the identification of the Yüeh-chou ware known from Chinese literary sources. As Brankston put it: 'Now we may see this colour of distant mountains and feel the winds and dew, for Yüeh ware has been dug up and is back among the living wares again.'

It is evident that a considerable interval of time separated the most active periods of the Tê-ch'ing/Chiu-yen kilns and of the kilns at Shang-lin-hu; typical products of Shang-lin-hu are not dissimilar in body material and glaze from those of the earlier kilns, but as Karlbeck states: 'there is a vast difference both in forms and patterns, and one cannot escape feeling that they belong to different epochs altogether.' The products of Shang-lin-hu also were exported in considerable quantity to such distant places as Persia and Egypt, where complete specimens or fragments have been found in modern times.

The evidence is fairly strong that the Shang-lin-hu potteries produced the original *pi-sê yao*, or 'secret colour ware', to which reference was made at the beginning of this chapter. However, Koyama has recently suggested that some Yüeh kilns at Yü-wang-miao, near Shao-hsing, may have made the highest-grade wares and *pi-sê yao*.[1] The Yü-wang-miao kilns were investigated in 1944 by a young Japanese scholar, Shigehiro Yoneda, who subsequently identified shards with finely incised decoration as having come from these sites; but it seems that no fragments were actually collected on the spot or brought back to substantiate this claim. Until further evidence is forthcoming, therefore, it seems safer to conclude that *pi-sê yao* was made at Shang-lin-hu, for the best Yüeh shards of which there is any reliable record have all come from this place.

According to J. M. Plumer, the Shang-lin-hu site was first visited by

---

[1] Fujio Koyama, 'The Yüeh-chou Yao Celadon excavated in Japan,' *Artibus Asiae*, Vol. XIV, 1–2, 1951. In this connection it is relevant to note that Sung records quoted in the *T'ao Shuo* and *T'ao Lu* state that *pi-sê yao* already existed in *T'ang* times, that it was made at Yüeh-chou (the old name for Shao-hsing) and that the kilns were moved to Yü-yao, some forty-five miles east of Shao-hsing, in the Southern Sung period. Shang-lin-hu is in Yü-yao hsien and about fifteen miles north of the town of Yü-yao, so that these records would seem to confirm that *pi-sê yao* was originally made at kilns close to Shao-hsing and only later transferred to Shang-lin-hu; however, not too much credence can be placed in Chinese ceramic literature, since the original works quoted often cannot be checked or their reliability proved; and it is quite likely that the location Yüeh-chou referred to the general area and not merely to the town of Shao-hsing. This was the conclusion reached by J. M. Plumer, who also explored the district; he notes that Chinese place-names often are applied to an extensive administrative region outside the city walls as well as to the area enclosed within and suggests that Yüeh-chou may be construed to mean the surrounding country even as far as Shang-lin-hu (James Marshall Plumer, 'Certain Celadon Potsherds from Samarra traced to their Source,' *Ars Islamica*, Vol. IV, 1937, p. 195).

a British missionary, Bishop Moule, in the early 1890's;[1] but no details of the kilns and their products seem to have become known until that indefatigable scholar, Dr. Manzō Nakao, found a clue to their location in the annals of Yü-yao hsien and despatched another Japanese, Mantaro Kaida, to investigate the area early in 1930. This exploratory trip must have called for some boldness on the part of Mr. Kaida, for the region was known to be a bandit stronghold; however, the results were beyond expectation, for the actual kiln sites were discovered and a considerable number of shards brought back. Most of these shards unfortunately were somewhat poor in quality and not a little doubt was expressed in Japan and elsewhere as to whether they could actually be Yüeh ware. However, Dr. Nakao sent some of the fragments to the British Museum, enabling Hobson to identify several complete specimens of Yüeh ware in English collections, and further study showed that such supremely beautiful examples as the large bowl in the Metropolitan Museum, New York, were essentially the same ware, though greatly superior in quality. Further expeditions were made to Shang-lin-hu and shards of better quality collected there.

Among the first of those following in Kaida's footsteps was the discoverer of the Tê-ch'ing kiln site, Tsuneo Yonaiyama. Subsequently the lake was visited by Yuzō Matsumura, Wan-li Chên, J. M. Plumer, A. D. Brankston and Manzō Nakao himself. One of the most vivid accounts of the scene is given by Yonaiyama, who writes:

'What a lovely lake this is! The mountain keeps its age-old calm; pink azaleas are in full blossom on its slopes and pine-trees stand here and there among the flowers. The exposed surface of the rock shines white. The lake is long and narrow, and reeds grow along its margin.

'On the shores there are kilns for making bricks. Clay is dug from the shallow parts of the lake and carried to the kilns by boat. It is a quiet spot, surrounded by mountains. On all sides are white rocks, green pine-trees, pink azaleas and the blue-green ranges. . . .

'About a dozen brick-kilns are scattered along the shores of the lake. They produce poorly-made bricks and roof-tiles. After it is brought across the lake by boat, the clay is piled up on the shore to dry. Pine-needles and pine-branches are used as fuel.

'At the southern end of the lake is a village of some twenty houses. . . . We landed from our boat and found that there was a narrow plain before reaching the foot of the mountain. The mountainside was covered with pine-trees and there were countless celadon shards scattered along the foothills and among the trees. We discovered old kiln sites all over the pine woods behind the village.

[1] James Marshall Plumer, 'Saggars of Sung—II,' *Oriental Art* (New Series), Vol. I, No. 2, Summer 1955, p. 77.

'In the vicinity of the village, too, there were numerous celadon shards. The area covered some twelve to fifteen acres along the foot of the mountain. However, there was no trace of the structure of the kilns to enable us to determine their number. At the foot of the pine-trees and in the cultivated fields, where the soil had been turned over, innumerable fragments of celadon could be seen, just like pebbles.'

On the eastern shores of the lake there was a small farmhouse, the walls of which had been built with fragments of celadon. The finest shards are said to have been found nearby. Describing this area, Matsumura states:

'The whole region as far as one could see was covered with pottery fragments, which must have run into millions. The sides of vessels—two or even three fused together at the base—spouts of ewers, bases of water-jars, large and small stilts, etc., all formed a deep stratum, putting one in mind of an ancient battlefield. Though poor in quality, they were all genuine Yü-yao ware. No one has yet found a perfect specimen. As an art-dealer who had brought many pieces to Hangchou complained, he could not find even slightly damaged specimens, let alone perfect ones.

'In this field of potsherds there were whole mounds formed by the fragments. To obtain data for students of ceramics, I looked for grave tablets and found two dating from the Han period and bearing inscriptions. . . .

'In front of a house in the village was a small inlet connecting with the lake, and a boat laden with wood-fuel was about to be unloaded. We could well imagine that, when the Yü-yao kilns were flourishing, pottery wares of all kinds would have been loaded on to just such small boats as this for shipment elsewhere, and it gave us quite a friendly feeling for the small boat, even though it was merely a poor sort of craft for the carrying of wood-fuel.'

It is perhaps unnecessary to describe the ware from Shang-lin-hu in any detail. Characteristic features such as the high, splayed foot-rim have been repeatedly mentioned and illustrated, and examples may be studied in the principal large collections in this country and elsewhere. Some typical specimens also are shown in the plates at the end of this book (I). However, a few remarks on their diversified decoration and on dating may be not without interest.

Most of the decoration of Shang-lin-hu ware was incised with a fine point, but Hobson was incorrect in stating that moulds did not appear to be used at Yü-yao for impressed designs: quite a number of specimens in the Ingram Collection and elsewhere as well as numerous

---

(I) *Plates* 10–18.

fragments exhibit elaborate moulded decoration (1). As might be expected of such an ardently Buddhist State as Wu-Yüeh, the lotus plays
a prominent part as a *motif* and one of the most frequent forms is the
wide-mouthed bowl with lotus-petals carved or moulded in relief
round the outside (2). Another design often found in relief and likewise carved or made with a mould is the dragon among waves or
clouds (3).There are several other kinds of relief ornament, but the full
richness of Yüeh decorative design is not apparent until one examines
the finely etched patterns adorning many of the bowls and dishes,
which—alas—often survive only in fragmentary condition (4). A
good idea of their variety and beauty may be obtained from the excellent study *Yüeh Ch'i T'u Lu,* published by Dr. Wan-li Chên in
1937, and the following passage from the English introduction seems
to have captured some of the freedom, vitality and naïveté of the designs themselves:

'The rich variety of designs on these wares is certainly unprecedented in the history of Chinese porcelain. Look at the butterflies flying
in pairs, the parrots and the phoenixes (5), the chirping birds among
the blossoms and the storks soaring high in the cloud. You have the
realistic portrayal of a wriggling loach or capering fish on a bowl, or
the fantastic picture of a twisting dragon in foaming waters on a
basin (6). On some you see four blooming lotus flowers shooting from
among the standing leaves, with a kingfisher flying among them.
What a wonderful decorative design! On some you have althaea
flowers and begonias beautifully incised. Even a diminutive and simple
ware may have on it some butterflies flitting among the blossoms.
These designs soon conduct the viewer to the realm of poetry and
painting, thrilling and satisfied. At the bottom of some plate you will
find the rushing bore of the Ch'ien-tang river and on the cover of a
small vessel peonies in full bloom . . . on certain broken pieces we also
find idealistic drawings of human figures.'

Certainly there had been nothing to equal these exquisite designs on
any earlier Chinese wares.

The princes of Wu-Yüeh ruled at Hangchou from 907 to 978, after
which the state was absorbed by the growing power of Sung. The passage which Dr. Nakao found in the local annals stated that Shang-lin-
hu formerly produced fine *pi-sê yao* and that government officials
were stationed there during the Sung period to supervise the kilns but
that this practice was later discontinued. Various inscriptions have

---

(1) Plate 18A; (2) *Plate 15, also Plate* 11B.
(3) *Plates 16 and 17;* (4) *Plates 12, 14 and 15;* (5) *Plates 12 and 15.*
(6) *Plates 16 and 17.*

been found, incised with a fine point under the glaze, on the base of shards collected at the site. Most of these are single characters and their meaning is obscure. Koyama lists fifteen, some of which he believes may refer to the cyclical year of make while others may be the first character of the name of a palace building. Some complete pieces with inscriptions are thought to be forgeries, but the manufacture of spurious fragments bearing inscriptions would seem to be both difficult and pointless. The inscription *T'ai P'ing Mou Yin* mentioned by Plumer occurs on many shards and signifies that the pieces concerned were made in the year 978. This was the actual date when Ch'ien Shu, Prince of Wu-Yüeh, abdicated in favour of the Sung Emperor. The historical records state that he journeyed to the Sung capital early in the year and was granted audience by the Emperor, subsequently accepting the status of a vassal. Thousands of porcelain wares—many having gold rims—were made for presentation to the Emperor in token of his submission: both the *Sung Shih* and *Sung Hui Yao* refer to a tributary offering of fifty thousand porcelains, of which one hundred and fifty were gilded. 'After this year,' states Koyama, 'the Yü-yao factory, which had been famed throughout the world for the manu-facture of Yüeh *pi-sê yao* under the patronage of the Ruling House of Wu-Yüeh, lost its protector and became an independent factory oper-ated by private individuals.'

Despite Matsumura's record of Han graves at Shang-lin-hu, it is un-likely that the potteries date back as far as this, but the discovery nearby of a celadon tablet bearing an epitaph dated the third year of Ch'ang-ch'ing, or 823, proves that the kilns were in operation during the T'ang period.[1] No doubt the finest wares were made during the Five Dynasties period and on into the early part of Sung, for not only did the State of Wu-Yüeh maintain its independence during the first eighteen years of the Sung period but, according to a passage in the *Sung Hui Yao* quoted by Dr. Chên, tribute in the form of porcelain wares continued to be paid to the Emperor at least until 1068. A somewhat puzzling reference in the *Liu Yen Chai Pi Chi* to *pi-sê yao* made at Yü-yao in the Southern Sung period states that the ware was 'coarse, plain and long-lasting';[2] further, that people thought it was made at official kilns. Koyama advises that he has never seen any celadon ware corresponding to this description, nor heard of any pieces from Shang-lin-hu thought to date from the Southern Sung; ac-cordingly he regards the accuracy of the record as very doubtful and

---

[1] Fujio Koyama, 'A Study of a T'ang Epitaph. . . .' (in Japanese), *Tōji*, Vol. VIII, No. 5, October 1936; an English translation of this article appeared in the *Far Eastern Ceramic Bulletin*, No. 12, December 1950.
[2] *T'ao Shuo*, p. 131 of Bushell's translation.

concludes that 'the best Yü-yao ware was made from late T'ang to the Five Dynasties, continuing to some extent into Sung but completely disappearing in Yüan and Ming'. The local annals, however, written about the seventeenth century, state: 'There are now private kilns in all the villages, but they mostly make poor quality wares such as un-glazed jars and pots', and no doubt the brick-kilns mentioned by Yonaiyama represent a continuation of the craft on a lower plane into modern times. After the fall of Wu-Yüeh there was probably a gradual drift away from Shang-lin-hu to the new and thriving potteries around K'ai-fêng and Lung-ch'üan, with the result that the kilns where the renowned *pi-sê yao* had been made degenerated into rural potteries or else were completely abandoned.

There is, however, a class of transitional T'ang/Sung ware of Yüeh type which cannot definitely be assigned to the Shang-lin-hu or other known potteries (1). In Japan as in the West this is generally regarded as Yüeh ware of the early Sung period, and most likely it was made at some factory in Chekiang province which has not yet been located. This would not exclude the view put forward by Dr. Chên that it is an early form of Lung-ch'üan ware, but on balance it has seemed best to con-sider it briefly in the chapter on Yüeh, to which it has an obvious affinity, although its exact origin remains obscure.[1] The body is a lighter grey than that of pottery from Shang-lin-hu, for which reason Sir Herbert Ingram has named it the 'grey ware'. It was fired in the normal Yüeh manner, either on a circular ring of clay or on three small lumps. The form and decoration show T'ang derivation, being split up and divided horizontally except on some specimens which seem to be of later date. The vases nearly always have two small loops on the shoulder beside the neck; their bodies are often divided into panels, usually five in number as in T'ang wares. However, a tall vase in the David Foundation bears an inscription dated the third year of Yüan Fêng, or 1080 (2), and the same date appears on a jar with five spouts in the Yamato Bunka Kan Collection in Osaka. Whatever its exact provenance, the 'grey ware' is among the most graceful of early Chinese porcelains; its elegance of form is complemented by a pale

[1] Dr. Chên writes: 'Among the pieces classified by foreigners as Yüeh ware there are some which should properly be called early Lung-ch'üan ware.' He proceeds to describe the type in question, maintaining that the early products of Lung-ch'üan 'had their origin in Yüeh ware' about the end of the Five Dynasties period and that 'as Yüeh ware declined, so did the Lung-ch'üan kilns begin to prosper'. Sir Herbert Ingram advises that Brankston also believed this class of ware came from the Lung-ch'üan area, but no definite evidence has been obtained from kiln sites. It seems to be transitional in type as in period and to be more closely allied to Yüeh than to any other known ware.

(1) *Plates* 19–22; (2) *Plate* 22.

bluish or greyish green glaze, so that some pieces have an almost white appearance.

The wide distribution of Yüeh ware throughout the Orient has already been mentioned: evidently it was a staple export during the T'ang period, when Chinese trade with the West grew to such large proportions and junks plied regularly between the China coast and the Persian Gulf. Arab writers from the ninth century onward refer to exports of Chinese porcelain, and the discovery of Yüeh fragments at Brahminabad in India, at Samarra on the River Tigris and at Fostât, the old city of Cairo, bear clear witness to the extent of the trade. References in early Japanese literature, notably in the 'Tales of Genji', to 'celadon' (*aoji* and *seiji*) and 'secret colour ware' (*hishoku*) show that Yüeh ware was known and highly prized in Japan under the Fujiwaras, or during the tenth and eleventh centuries, and there is good evidence that the development of Korean celadon about the middle of the eleventh century took place with the assistance of potters from Yüeh, who may have settled in southern Korea as a result of inducements offered by the rising kingdom of Koryo.[1] Several specimens of Yüeh ware have been found in Korean tombs, but a few examples discovered in Japan are of more significance, the earliest being an incense-jar preserved from the eighth century among the treasures of Hōryūji Temple, near Nara; a three-legged pot excavated from the site of the provincial government of western Japan during the same period, in the vicinity of Fukuoka, cannot be much later in date, while two small Yüeh vessels from Ninnaji Temple in Kyoto were found buried under a shrine which is known to have been erected in the year 904. The finest Yüeh specimen found in Japan is probably the ewer from Kobata, near Kyoto, which was excavated at the site of a temple built in 1005 and used as the cemetery of the Fujiwara clan during the eleventh and twelfth centuries (1).

The discovery of Chinese celadon fragments at Samarra on the River Tigris was made by Dr. Friedrich Sarre in 1913, and it has since become evident that the fragments are of Yüeh ware from the Shang-lin-hu potteries.[2] Samarra was the capital of the Abbasid Caliphs from 836 to 883, when it was abandoned and fell into ruins, and most of the

---

[1] For a comparative study of Yüeh ware and Koryo celadon see the author's article: 'The "Kingfisher Celadon" of Koryo,' *Artibus Asiae*, Vol. XVI, 1953, pp. 14–24. The earliest Korean celadons were clearly modelled on Yüeh ware: the shapes were often the same, the decoration similarly incised with a fine point, or else moulded, with the use of identical *motifs*, and details of technique were closely copied.

[2] James Marshall Plumer, *op. cit.* (*Ars Islamica*).

(1) *Plate* 13.

wares imported from China are believed to have arrived during this period, though a few later specimens also were found. The city of Fostât likewise reached its zenith in the late ninth century under Ibn Tulun, who was brought up in Samarra and arrived as Governor in 864; the city was destroyed in 1169 and, although subsequently rebuilt, declined in importance and finally became a rubbish dump. A vast number of ceramic fragments have been found at the site, and these include many later Chinese wares as well as local products; among the earlier fragments, however, are many fine specimens of Yüeh ware dating from the T'ang and Five Dynasties periods.[1]

It would thus seem that a few examples of Yüeh ware reached neighbouring countries during the eighth century, but the period when it became a major export probably began early in the ninth and continued through the T'ang dynasty and on into the early part of Sung.

[1] The discoveries at Fostât have been discussed in several articles, among which the following may be cited: R. L. Hobson, 'Chinese Porcelain from Fostât,' *The Burlington Magazine*, Vol. LXI, August 1932; Leigh Ashton, 'China and Egypt,' *O.C.S. Transactions*, Vol. 11, 1933-4.

3

SOME UNIDENTIFIED CELADONS— FROM T'ANG TO SUNG

Although the great majority of pre-Sung celadons seem to have been made at one or other of the Yüeh kilns, a number of specimens in English, American and Japanese collections do not fit in with any known type and remain subjects for speculation. Most of these pieces exhibit strong T'ang characteristics and seem unlikely to have been made after the tenth century; others from their shape and style may be more appropriately classed as early Sung. There are no convincing reasons for assigning them to kilns which are known solely from brief references in the Chinese literature, and their scarcity usually precludes any attempt to classify them into groups. Attention will here be confined to a few examples of special interest and to one more common type for which a very tentative attribution is suggested. It will be admitted, however, that there is at present no sure means of identifying the specimens discussed, or even of determining with any certainty the part of China in which they were made.

One of the earliest of these specimens is a globular water-pot on three small feet—a well-known T'ang shape—in the Ingram Collection at Oxford which has a dark, almost black, body and a bluish green glaze of very soft appearance (1); this piece is said to have come from North China and there is no reason for supposing that it was made any later than the T'ang period, but it foreshadows very clearly the subtle qualities of form and colour which came to be associated especially with Sung wares.

A very different kind of T'ang celadon is represented by a small bowl in the collection of Sir Alan Barlow which has engraved lotus-petal decoration under a light olive-green glaze (2). Similar examples in Japan are regarded as Hung-chou ware; however, this attribution does not rest on a very secure basis. Koyama mentions that two specimens were acquired by a Japanese collector at Nan-ch'ang, the modern

(1) *Plate* 23B; (2) *Plate* 23A.

name for Hung-chou, in Kiangsi province, but the kiln site, which was reported to be in the outskirts of the town, could not be investigated owing to the hostilities then taking place between Chinese and Japanese forces. Dr. Chên states that no proof has yet been discovered of the location of this kiln. Hung-chou ware is mentioned in the celebrated 'Tea Classic' by the T'ang writer Lu Yü. The 'Tea Classic' also refers to the celadon wares of Ting-chou, Wu-chou, Shou-chou and Yo-chou, but only the last-named of these potteries has so far been reliably located—near Yo-yang (or Yo-chou) in Hunan province. According to Dr. Chên, the products were much inferior to Yüeh ware, but some of the 'Yo-chou pottery' recently acquired in Hongkong has considerable charm and seems to show close kinship with Yüeh.[1]

A number of indeterminate celadons of early date are often assigned somewhat arbitrarily to one of the better-known categories—usually to Northern Celadon or Yüeh—although it cannot be maintained that they present the distinctive features associated with these wares (I). They include numerous funerary jars as well as several kinds of vase. The glaze often has a decidedly olive tinge, but sometimes it is pale green. Sir Herbert Ingram has called attention to one feature which many of these pieces have in common: the glaze has been wiped or roughly scraped from the base before the firing took place. It seems probable that this 'scraped base ware' was all made at a particular factory; examples are generally heavy and solidly built, and the shapes are characteristic: 'One of the most typical is the funeral vase with cover, five spouts and what may be aptly described as a series of fat rolls on the body. When they had finished with the fat rolls the remainder of the body was almost always decorated with long upright leaves and the foot-rims were usually of the T'ang type.'[2]

There has been equal uncertainty in Japan concerning the provenance of the 'scraped base' and allied wares. One suggestion is that they were made at Li-shui, between Lung-ch'üan and Ch'u-chou in southern Chekiang. According to the T'ao Lu, Li-shui ware was made in the Sung period and somewhat resembled Lung-ch'üan ware, though some pieces were dark and others light. The body was coarse and thick and the workmanship poor. Koyama believes that the early Sung Li-shui kilns made celadon ware with a northern or olive-coloured glaze and relief decoration carved underneath:

[1] See Dr. Isaac Newton's paper, 'Some Coloured and White Wares from Hunan,' O.C.S. Transactions, Vol. 27, 1951–3, pp. 28–9.

[2] Sir Herbert Ingram, 'Form: an important factor in the dating of early Chinese ceramics,' Ethnos, No. 4, 1946, p. 162.

(I) Plates 24–7.

'The Northern Sung Li-shui ware seems to have closely resembled Northern Celadon, both wares exhibiting the influence of Yüeh ware from Yü-yao; their glaze and body are so alike that they can hardly be differentiated, but the shapes and style are dissimilar. In a word, Northern Sung Li-shui ware is not as sharply or clearly defined as Northern Celadon and seems to date from an earlier period. It seems that the early kiln sites were found some years ago near the capital of Li-shui hsien, and Dr. Chên as well as a few others visited them, but no details have yet been published.' Sir Herbert Ingram stresses the T'ang flavour of the 'scraped base ware', but there is a typical Sung elegance about some of the vases and these are generally considered to date from the early part of Sung. Probably the ware originated in the T'ang period and continued through the Five Dynasties into the Sung.[1]

Some mention should be made of perhaps the most mysterious of all early Chinese wares—the Ch'ai porcelain made in the reign of the Emperor Shih Tsung (954–9), said to be 'as blue as the sky, as clear as a mirror, as thin as paper, as resonant as a musical stone'. This was a Palace ware made specially to the order of the Emperor, who commanded that its colour should be 'the blue of the sky after rain as seen in rifts of the clouds'.[2] According to the fourteenth-century *Ko Ku Yao Lun*, it was made at Chêng-chou, near K'ai-fêng, and was 'rich, refined and unctuous, with fine crackle and, in many cases, coarse yellow clay on the foot'. By the sixteenth century it was 'no longer to be found' and fragments were greatly treasured, being mounted into bracelets and buckles like precious stones. Fabulous powers were often ascribed to these.

Reputed specimens of Ch'ai ware in the Peking Palace and other

---

[1] Perhaps the designation Li-shui ware, even as a tentative attribution, is hardly justified on so flimsy a basis; but the time has come for a determined effort to be made to place in a separate category wares which can no longer be regarded as Northern Celadon despite a certain superficial resemblance. Originally Northern Celadon was the vague generic term given to all specimens of celadon which differed from Lung-ch'üan ware and had a slight olive tinge; later it was found that most if not all the examples of Yüeh ware in English and American collections had been included in this amorphous group, but no further steps have been taken to break down what is clearly an arbitrary classification into which some heterogeneous types have been thrown. As will be seen in the next chapter, Northern Celadon is a very distinctive ware, whatever may be its identity; it was made at a group of potteries, probably extending over quite a large area, in northern Honan, and it presents certain clear-cut features which cannot be found in some of the specimens still bearing the same name—though largely, it would seem, for lack of any other attribution.

[2] The *T'ao Lu* refers to the colour of Ju ware as 'approaching the blue of the sky after rain' but admits that this epithet is properly applicable only to Ch'ai. It is generally assumed from this and other indications that Ch'ai, like Ju, was a type of celadon.

collections differ from one another and do not correspond with the traditional description; in fact no satisfactory identification of Ch'ai has ever been made, and it must be assumed that the ware no longer exists. Koyama describes the literary records as 'empty phrases' and concludes that 'Ch'ai ware remains a complete mystery'. Count Otani goes further, suggesting that Ch'ai ware was 'a figment of the imagination developed in the Ming period'. He points out that the literature on Ch'ai all dates from the Ming period or later, that use of the ruler's family name—Ch'ai—for a pottery ware seems most unlikely and that Shih Tsung's short reign was fully occupied with wars and expeditions, so that 'there was no time for the construction of kilns'.[1] Furthermore, no satisfactory explanation can be found for the disappearance of Ch'ai or the substitution of Ting as the Imperial ware. Dr. Chên likewise considers it questionable that official kilns were established by the Emperor at Chêng-chou and mentions another theory derived from a passage in the annals of Yü-yao hsien. This quotes an earlier source to the effect that Ch'ai was the name given to superior Yüeh ware, or *pi-sê yao*, when it was presented to the Court during the reign of Shih Tsung. It is thus possible that the tradition refers to a special order given by the Emperor for porcelains to be made at the Yüeh factory and that these became known by the family name of the ruler for whom they were produced.

It seems unlikely that the mystery of Ch'ai will ever be solved unless, as Hobson put it, 'a lucky excavator should some day light on a buried piece'.

[1] Kōzui Otani, *Shina Kō-tōji* (Ancient Chinese Pottery), Tokyo, 1932. It should be noted that Shih Tsung was Emperor of the Later Chou, the last of the Five Dynasties, and that his dominion extended only from the Khitan frontier in the vicinity of Peking as far as the Yangtze. In the year 960 General Chao K'uang-yin, commanding the Imperial forces of the Later Chou, became Emperor and founded the Sung dynasty.

4

JU AND OTHER NORTHERN
WARES

The inclusion of Ju ware among Chinese celadons may occasion some surprise, as already indicated in the Introduction. The Chinese literature normally refers to ceramic wares by their place of origin, calling Ju ware 'the porcelain of Ju-chou', and the modern practice of using descriptive terms like celadon has not in the West been extended to such famous wares as Ju, although there has been no hesitation to do so in China and Japan. However, the true nature of Ju ware was clearly recognized by Hobson at least twenty years before it became possible to identify the few specimens, 'rare as stars at dawn', in English collections. Hobson wrote: '. . . the celebrated Ju Chou ware was evidently of the grey green celadon type, with perhaps a tinge of blue, like the early Corean wares', and again: '. . . we may conclude that the Ju porcelain was a beautiful ware of celadon type, varying in tint from a very pale green to a bluish green.'[1]

Hobson based this conclusion primarily on the important record of Hsü Ching, a Chinese scholar who accompanied the Sung envoy to Korea in the year 1123 and wrote a graphic account of the country on his return to China. Hsü Ching described the ceramic wares made by the Koreans and was particularly impressed by the beauty of their celadon glaze and the novelty of some of their designs. After giving details of one of the most striking—an incense burner with a crouching lion on its cover—he remarked: 'the rest bear a general resemblance to the old *pi-sê* ware of Yüeh-chou and the new kiln wares of Ju-chou'. The similarity of the earliest Korean celadons to Yüeh ware has already been noted, and it has become evident in recent years that Hsü Ching's second comparison was no less apt. [2]

---

[1] R. L. Hobson, *Chinese Pottery and Porcelain*, Vol. I, pp. 42 and 54.

[2] See p. 20, footnote 1. Hsü Ching states that a great improvement had taken place shortly before his visit, especially in the colour and glaze. Specimens of the types he describes have survived: not only are these greatly superior to the Yüeh-style wares which preceded them, but they often bear a startling resemblance to the ware now identified as Ju.

Unfortunately this Korean association led to a mistaken theory propounded by Mr. Eumorfopoulos that *ying-ch'ing* ware,[1] most of which at the time was being recovered from Korean tombs, was—if not Ju itself—at least of Ju type, and this view gained such currency for some years that Hobson's descriptions of *ying-ch'ing* specimens in the Eumorfopoulos Collection all give the attribution 'Ju type'. It was not until the publication of Sir Percival David's valuable monograph on Ju ware[2] soon after the great Exhibition of Chinese Art in London that the problem was resolved to the satisfaction of most Western students and collectors. Authenticated specimens of Ju ware loaned by the Chinese Government and by Sir Percival David himself were on view at the Exhibition.

It is disconcerting to note that an entirely different conception of Ju ware obtains in Japan, and also to some extent in China, where the class widely known as Northern Celadon has been identified as Ju. This view is based on the discovery of Northern Celadon shards at kiln sites in the vicinity of Lin-ju hsien, the modern name for Ju-chou, especially by a Japanese Buddhist priest, Gentotsu Harada. Acting on instructions from Count Otani and braving the perils of attack by brigands, Harada explored six kiln sites, four at Chang-hsieh li and one each at Ku-i li and Kuei-jên li, collecting several score fragments. These are described by Koyama as being mainly Northern Celadon but also including Chün ware, white ware of Tz'u-chou type and 'some entirely different celadon ware.' The number of places mentioned in the local annals as having some connection with pottery making runs to well over thirty, so that the investigation cannot be regarded as thorough: indeed Harada was able to spend only a few days in the area. His account, published in a Japanese newspaper shortly after his journey,[3] indicates the reasons for haste and is perhaps of sufficient interest to be worth quoting in part:

'On the morning of March 7th. I pressed on with great determination toward an area infested with brigands. Since there were no horse-carts in this region, I had to travel on horseback. I did not know how to ride a horse, so I had to practise immediately before starting. Then, with the aid of a groom, I mounted my steed and set off. The path was very hazardous, with outcrops of bare rock and crags, not to mention narrow tracks following the courses of streams. On the way I encountered donkeys carrying coal, and thus I knew that the early kiln sites were near at hand. I reached my destination at about two o'clock

---

[1] More correctly termed *ch'ing pai*.

[2] Sir Percival David, 'A Commentary on Ju Ware,' *O.C.S. Transactions*, Vol. 14, 1936–7.

[3] Tokyo Nichi Nichi, April 13th, 1931.

and indulged in a cup of tea at a farmhouse beside the way. Looking inside, I noticed two old-fashioned muskets. I realized that these people, too, had to protect themselves against brigands—or perhaps they sometimes turned brigands themselves. I was surprised when they asked me whether there were guns in Japan. The village had been attacked by brigands several times and was in a state of ruin. Behind it was a cave that could hold two or three hundred people and had embrasures for guns. When the villagers told me that this was a place of refuge in case of attack by brigands, I felt very sorry for them.

'On cultivated land some three Chinese *li* from the village I found scattered remains of bricks used in high-temperature firing, coal cinders and early shards. I started digging immediately and found many fragments of pottery wares. For once in my life I felt that my hardships had been rewarded. As Count Otani had told me, there were coal mines, clay suitable for pottery making and a clear stream, all of which served to confirm that this was an early kiln site. . . . On the morning of 11th, I collected more fragments at other early kiln sites and, on my return, learned that about one hundred brigands had attacked a village some 60 *li* distant. The headmen of neighbouring hamlets called an emergency meeting to discuss what steps should be taken, and the people were very alarmed and urged me to return to Lin-ju hsien. Further exploration became impossible, so I made my way to Lin-ju hsien and was kept busy all night packing up my collection of shards. . . .'

Previous to Harada's investigations that enterprising Japanese scholar, Dr. Nakao, believed that Ju ware was a white porcelain not unlike Ting. Conflicting accounts in the Chinese records had, in Japan as elsewhere, resulted in widely different interpretations and general confusion. However, like other Japanese authorities, Dr. Nakao became convinced by Harada's finds that the chief product of the Ju-chou kilns was Northern Celadon. Apparently he later visited the Ju-chou sites himself, for he sent three fragments he had collected there to the British Museum, two being of Chün type and one Northern Celadon, with the result that Hobson also considered it reasonable to regard the Ju-chou district as a likely provenance of Northern Celadon.[1]

After studying Harada's shards, Count Otani evolved the theory that there had been a chronological development of Ju ware. Hsü Ching's record referred to the 'new kiln wares of Ju-chou' and therefore left no room for doubt that the kilns had been established in the early part of the twelfth century, but Otani now suggested that it im-

[1] R. L. Hobson, 'Yüeh Ware and Northern Celadon,' *O.C.S. Transactions*, Vol. 14, 1936–7, p. 17.

plied the existence of older kilns. He believed that the earliest kilns in the Ju-chou district were probably rural potteries making white wares in common with other local factories in North China, but supposed that these were succeeded by the 'old kilns', which made the 'sky-blue' Chün type, while toward the end of the Northern Sung period new kilns were set up for the production of celadon ware. Otani's theory was supported by Baron Ozaki, who identified the Chün type as the class often called 'Kuan Chün' by Western scholars and claimed that it was the official ware made for use at the Palace, while the later products of the new kilns were said to be Northern Celadon.[1] Recent Japanese studies have modified this conception only by abandoning the idea of succession: thus, Koyama points out that there is no reason to suppose that there were any older Ju kilns—Hsü Ching was merely contrasting the contemporary wares of Ju-chou with the antique Yüeh *pi-sê* ware—but considers that there were two classes of Ju ware made at the same period. The first of these was the superior type for the service of the Palace, which was produced for only a short time and has always been exceedingly rare, and the second was the commoner ware known as Northern Celadon and made for use by the general populace. Koyama agrees that the pieces identified as Ju in the West are official Ju porcelains made for the Palace; he considers 'Kuan Chün' to be another variety of official Ju, supporting to this extent the view strongly held by Ozaki,[2] but places both in a special category distinct from the others, i.e. Northern Celadon, which he regards as the ordinary type of Ju.

In reaching these conclusions it is clear that Japanese scholars were particularly influenced by two considerations, the first being that the only field studies in the Ju-chou district had been carried out by reputable fellow-countrymen and had resulted in the discovery of high-grade Chün and Northern Celadon shards, and the second that the resemblance of many Korean celadon bowls with moulded decoration to similar Northern Celadon bowls was well known. A number of Northern Celadon bowls had, indeed, been found in Korean tombs of the Koryo period, roughly contemporaneous with the Sung, and were for many years taken to be Korean celadons: the Korean Archaeological Survey illustrates both kinds of ware and makes no distinction between them, though the error has long since been recognized.[3] It

[1] Junsei Ozaki, 'Sung and Yüan Ceramic Wares' (in Japanese), *Tōki Kōza*, 24, 1938. See translation of the section on Ju ware by R. T. Paine in *Far Eastern Ceramic Bulletin*, September 1948 and March 1949.

[2] Junsei Ozaki, *op. cit.* See also the same writer's article, 'On the "Sê Ch'ing Tai Fên Hung" of the Southern Sung Kuan-yao' in *Tōsetsu*, March and June 1954, translated in *Far Eastern Ceramic Bulletin*, December 1955.

[3] Fujio Koyama, 'The Ancient Ceramic Wares of Koryo' (in Japanese), *Tōki*

should be added that Japanese scholars have had little opportunity for studying at first hand the ware identified as Ju in the West, for the only specimen of this type which has turned up in Japan escaped notice until the end of 1953 (1). On the other hand, Japanese collections have long contained a number of Northern Celadons of outstanding size and quality, comparable to the larger and more striking specimens of Ting ware. Japanese students therefore had some exceptionally fine examples of Northern Celadon available for examination but were compelled to rely mainly on illustrations for their study of the Ju wares owned by the Chinese Government and a few English collectors. This may also explain why the latter have not gained recognition in Japan as a separate type, distinguishable from 'Kuan Chün'. However, leaving the question of Northern Celadon for later consideration, it will now be shown that the Japanese and Western conceptions of official Ju are not far apart.

One of the most remarkable ceramic 'documents' in existence is the ritual disc in the David Foundation which bears an incised inscription to the effect that it was the first piece to be made at the official factory at Ju-chou on April 9th, 1107 (2). The authenticity of this important relic will always, perhaps, be open to question, for not only does it differ somewhat in glaze and style from other examples of Ju ware but the inscription is very circumstantial and the odds against survival of so unique a specimen must have been considerable. However, there are substantial grounds for accepting it at face value, one being that the supervisor of the factory is named in the inscription and has been traced in the *Sung Shih* and other historical records, the details of his career being in no way inconsistent with such an appointment. If its validity is accepted, it establishes the exact date when the Ju kilns began making official wares for the Palace. Accordingly it is hard to resist the conclusion reached by Sir Percival David and also, it would seem, by Baron Ozaki[1] that the 'Northern Kuan' mentioned in the Chinese literature could not at this period have been anything but Ju. In support of this view is an early record that the Kuan kilns were established at the capital, now known as K'ai-fêng, in the Chêng Ho era (1111–17), while a later authority places it in the Ta Kuan (1107–11). This was the very time when official Ju ware was being made either at Ju-chou or 'within the forbidden precincts of the Palace enclosure'—

Kōza, 1937. Koyama lists the following illustrations of Northern Celadons in the Korean Archaeological Survey, *Chōsen Koseki Zufu*, Vol. 8: Nos. 3450, 3475–8, 3480–2, 3486.

[1] Junsei Ozaki, *op. cit.* (*Tōki Kōza*), section on Kuan ware. Ozaki's conclusion, like Sir Percival David's, is based mainly on sinological grounds.

(1) *Plate* 33; (2) *Plate* 28A.

as suggested by one rendering of a twelfth-century text.[1] On the other hand, it is difficult to reconcile the theory that Ju and Northern Kuan were the same with the distinction which seems to be made in the Chinese literature between Ju ware and all Kuan ware, whether Northern or Southern, and it is at least surprising that no indication is given of the terms being used synonymously.

Another theory held by some Western scholars is that various types of ware were made at the official factory at different times, or even at the same time, and all known as Northern Kuan. Koyama refers to a suggestion along these lines which was made to him by Dr. Ferguson in Peking: 'He stated that, as the Northern Kuan kilns were established at the capital and operated directly by the Government, several kinds of ware may have been made by skilled potters from the Ju, Ting and Tz'u-chou kilns whom the Government hired, with material gathered from all over the country.' Sir Percival David also has inclined some way toward this view: thus, after mentioning with approval Hobson's description of a small jar in the Eumorfopoulos Collection as 'Kuan Chün', he goes on to refer to a brush washer owned by Sir Alan Barlow, which has a soft lavender glaze, as 'another and an outstanding specimen of this type of ware, partly Chün and partly Ju in character, but best classified, I think, as Northern Kuan'.[2] It will be noted that this conception, however, restricts the area of choice from the wide range suggested by Dr. Ferguson to wares of the Ju and Chün type. The connection between Ju and the finer class of Chün is, indeed, now realized to be much closer than was formerly thought, and it seems very probable that the wares made for the Palace included some that approximated in style to high-grade Chün. This would certainly have been the case if some of the potters employed at the Kuan kilns had actually been recruited from the Chün-chou potteries, located about half-way between K'ai-fêng and Ju-chou, and it would explain the superior type of Chün ware, which Hobson felt it proper to class as Kuan and Ozaki considers to be a product of the official Ju kilns but none the less identifiable as Northern Kuan.

There remains the possibility that Northern Kuan may have been a special type of ware originating at K'ai-fêng. The official factory may have set up at Ju-chou in 1107, as stated on the ritual disc, and later transferred to the capital. This may have been done for reasons of convenience or because efforts were to be made to produce a class of ware superior even to Ju, probably by eclectic methods but on the basis of another local product which had gained favour, such as Tung.

[1] Sir Percival David, *op. cit.* p. 26.
[2] Sir Percival David, Introduction to *O.C.S. Catalogue of an Exhibition of Ju and Kuan Wares*, reprinted in *O.C.S. Transactions*, Vol. 27, 1951-3.

Though nowhere stated explicitly, this hypothesis is in conformity with the literary evidence, which indicates that Northern Kuan was not dissimilar, though much superior, to Tung ware and that both were celadons, with 'brown mouth and iron foot' and some fine crackle or crazing.[1]

We shall return briefly to the question of Northern Kuan but at this point note merely that there has been some convergence in the Japanese and Western viewpoints on official Ju; the real point at issue continues to be the Japanese identification of Northern Celadon as the ordinary, or mass-produced, type of Ju.

The chief argument put forward against this Japanese concept has been the well-established fact that Ju ware was always extremely rare. If there is one point concerning Ju on which all the Chinese literary sources agree, it is that the ware was official, or Imperial, and consequently most difficult to procure, even in early times. Thus the *Ch'ing Po Tsa Chih*, a record of Sung affairs written in 1192, refers to the ware as follows:

'Ju ware was made exclusively for the Palace. . . . Pieces rejected for use at the Palace were sold in the market, but they are very hard to obtain. . . .'

The only specimen of Ju ware mentioned in the *T'ao Shuo*, among many examples of other famous wares, was a small vessel described by Li Jih-hua about the end of the sixteenth century as follows:

'At the time (Ju ware) was made solely for the Emperor's use, and consequently it is very difficult to procure a specimen. When I was Governor of Ju-chou, I saw only a single piece, a miniature jar in the home of Wên, a high-ranking military officer. . . .'

On the more doubtful authority of Hsiang Yüan-pien's Album, which originated at about the same time, we learn that very few products of the Ju-chou kilns were still in existence and that surviving specimens were mostly cups and dishes, often in damaged or imperfect condition. A few years later another writer declared that Ju porcelains were as extinct as the legendary Ch'ai.

The exact sense of Chinese texts is not always clear, with the result that different interpretations are often given, but there cannot be much doubt as to the special nature and excessive rarity of Ju ware. This fact is clearly recognized by Ozaki, yet no Japanese authority seems to have regarded the abundance, even in our own time, of Northern Celadon

[1] The *T'ao Shuo* states that Tung porcelain 'resembles the Imperial ware of the Sung dynasty'. Quoting the *Ko Ku Yao Lun*, published in 1387, it states: 'It is of pale green colour marked with fine crackle lines and has usually a brown mouth and iron-coloured foot. When compared with the Imperial ware of the period it wants red colour, the form is more clumsy and the paste is less finely worked and opaque.'

as weakening the case for its identification as Ju; nor can it be claimed that extant specimens of Northern Celadon are all excavated pieces which were unknown to later generations of Chinese. It is, of course, well known that Ting was an official ware, preceding Ju, and that, besides the pieces made or selected for the Palace, a vast production was organized for general use. Probably this fact has influenced the Japanese viewpoint on Ju. But the circumstances seem to have been quite different, for the tradition based on records going back to the twelfth century is that the Emperor became dissatisfied with Ting on account of certain imperfections and ordered a factory to be set up at Ju-chou to make celadon (ch'ing) ware. It is clear that this was done with a view to supplying the needs of the Palace, and the references given above confirm that Ju ware was not generally available to the public. It has been assumed by Western students that there were potteries at Ju-chou making Ju prototypes before the Imperial command was given, and several likely examples of this precursory Ju ware are known, but there are no grounds for believing that production was at any time on the scale of Ting or Northern Celadon. It is sometimes claimed by Japanese students who recognize the force of this argument that use of the name Ju to describe Northern Celadon is in any case justified on the basis that it was made in the Ju-chou district, and this also appears to be the current practice in China;[1] however, it is not in conformity with the Chinese literature, which confines the name to the official ware of classic fame and never refers to any other kind of Ju-chou porcelain. Moreover, there are grounds for believing that Northern Celadon, like Chün, was made in other parts of Honan province besides Ju-chou.

There is another strong reason for regarding the specimens of Ju ware in English collections as authentic and representative, and that is the astonishing resemblance they bear, in form, style and glaze, to the earlier Korean celadons dating from about the time of Hsü Ching's visit. The similarity between the two wares is, indeed, so great that it would be easy at first glance to mistake a group of Ju porcelains for Korean celadons and vice versa. Even after careful examination there

---

[1] While there can never have been much doubt among Chinese experts on the question of official Ju, accepted examples of which were sent to London by the Peking Palace authorities for the International Exhibition of Chinese Art, it seems that current Chinese opinion as expressed by Dr. Chên supports the Japanese view that Northern Celadon is another type of Ju ware. Dr. Chên states that Lin-ju hsien was the centre, kilns to the north-east making the earlier celadons, which were a fine green colour with 'broken ice crackle' but had no decoration, while kilns established later to the south used carved and impressed floral decoration. 'The ruling class of that time knew that the Lin-ju potters were highly skilled and included many excellent craftsmen; as a result the Lin-ju workers were selected to display their skill and developed what is known as official Ju ware.'

is sometimes uncertainty concerning the attribution in particular cases. In the face of this remarkable affinity, the fact that certain Korean bowls have impressed or carved decoration which was obviously copied from Northern Celadon—just as others show imitations of Ting and *ying-ch'ing* designs—pales into insignificance. The Koreans clearly did not follow the strongly individual shapes of Northern Celadon,[1] where-as they seem to have found the easy gracefulness of Ju ware very much to their taste. Korean ceramic forms reached their peak, largely under the influence of Ju ware, in the first half of the twelfth century, after which increased preoccupation with decorative patterns brought about a gradual decline.

The identification of Ju ware in the West is, of course, based on many other factors which need not be considered here, since a very thorough examination of the question will be found in Sir Percival David's monograph mentioned earlier. However, it will not be out of place to set down briefly the distinctive characteristics of Ju ware, as exemplified by specimens in the David Foundation and elsewhere.[2] It is made of buff stoneware, well composed but rather soft in type and having a dull resonance. Sir Harry Garner has described it as more like pottery than porcelain, possibly as a result of its being fired at a lower temperature than was customary for Sung porcelain. The glaze is a smooth, opaque bluish green, often with a tinge of lavender, and usually covers the entire vessel, but there is some variation in the

---

[1] The specimens illustrated in Plates 40, 43, 50A, 52B are quite alien in form to Korean celadon ware.

[2] A list of known specimens of Ju ware in collections outside China and Formosa may be of interest and is given below:

Percival David Foundation		14 pieces	(including the ritual disc but excluding 2 miniatures and 8 fragments)
British Museum	3	,,	(two damaged by fire)
Mrs. Alfred Clark	2	,,	
Sir Harry Garner	2	,,	
Röhss Museum, Gothenburg	2	,,	
City Art Gallery, Bristol	1	,,	
Musée Guimet, Paris	1	,,	
Sir Alan Barlow	1	,,	
Museum of Art, Philadelphia	1	,,	
City Museum, St. Louis	1	,,	
Mr. Stephen Juncunc, Chicago	1	,,	
Royal Ontario Museum, Toronto	1	,,	
Mr. Yasunari Kawabata, Kamakura	1	,,	
	31		

Ten specimens from the Peking Palace Museum also were shown at the International Exhibition of Chinese Art in London in 1935–6.

B. *Ju Ware. Vase with pear-shaped body and tapering neck,*
flaring at the mouth.
Sung dynasty. Height 8 in.
Mrs. Alfred Clark. See page 55

colour and in the type of crackle.[1] Characteristic features are the clearly defined, slightly splayed foot-rim and the three or more small oval spur marks on the base (I). Sometimes, however, the foot-rim is omitted, as in the case of two elliptical brush washers in the David Foundation, and the spur marks may be missing or less neatly executed. It should be noted that similar spur marks became the distinctive sign of Korean celadons: at first they were carried out with a care and skill equal to that of Ju, but later they became rough and irregular as the ware slowly coarsened and declined.

Above all else Ju ware is distinguished by its fine potting and the superb quality of its glaze. Despite individual variations in both glaze and crackle—shown also in some fragments in the David Foundation which are believed to have served as test pieces in the kilns—there is a marked general consistency of type. It is impossible to examine and handle surviving specimens without becoming convinced that here, if anywhere, is one of the classic Sung wares, simple of form, perfectly proportioned and outstandingly beautiful in colour and glaze (2).

But even if we consider the identity of Ju ware no longer in doubt, there remains the awkward corollary question concerning the nature and provenance of Northern Celadon. For here we have an extremely fine ware clearly dating from the Northern Sung period and surviving in abundance, yet apparently never praised or even described in the Chinese records. If we reject the Japanese theory that Northern Celadon is the common type of Ju ware, how are we to explain this anomaly?

The term Northern Celadon has never been regarded as anything but vague and unsatisfactory; yet, as Hobson pointed out, it has a certain literary and regional sanction, being associated with the Tung celadon ware of the north and generally found in that part of China. Tung ware is stated in the *T'ao Lu* to have been made in Chên-liu, a few miles south-east of K'ai-fêng, and fragments of Northern Celadon are said to have been excavated at this place.[2] However, we have seen

---

[1] Sometimes the crackle has a peculiar flaky texture resembling broken ice (see Plate 28B) or—as described by Nils Palmgren—'forming small angular fields, almost like scales, where the outlines are often doubled or trebled'. (Nils Palmgren, 'Two Ju Yao Dishes in Gothenburg,' *Röhsska Konstslöjdmuseet*, Årstryck, 1952, p. 38). A similar effect is found, but only rarely, on Kuan and other celadon wares; probably it was caused by some difference in contraction between the glaze and body either during or after firing. All the examples of Ju ware listed in footnote 2 on p. 34 are undecorated with the exception of a brush washer in the David Foundation, which has a lightly impressed floral design.

[2] By Kuo Pao Ch'ang. See Hobson in *O.C.S. Transactions*, Vol. 14, 1936-7, p. 15.

(I) *Plate 33*; (2) *Plates 28–33 and Colour Plate B.*

that many Northern Celadon shards were found in the vicinity of Ju-chou, and Mr. Basil Gray is probably correct in surmising that the ware was made at several potteries in the northern part of Honan province, whereas the references to Tung ware suggest a more local and a rarer product. Sir Percival David has proposed several pieces in the David Foundation and elsewhere as likely examples of Tung ware,[1] and there is good reason to accept this attribution at least tenta-tively; but his view that the ware later developed into Northern Cela-don at present lacks the support of sufficient evidence. A beautiful ewer with strongly carved decoration and a soft, bluish green glaze is regarded by Japanese authorities as a probable specimen of Tung: the somewhat coarse, greyish body conforms with literary descriptions of the ware, while the striking effect is consistent with fabrication at one of the more celebrated northern kilns (1). An even more impressive example of the same kind is to be seen at the Museum of Art, Cleve-land (2), and there are similar ewers in the Museum of Fine Arts, Boston, and in the collection of Lord Cunliffe (3).

After visiting K'ai-fêng and devoting some time to discussions with local scholars, Koyama reached the conclusion that the Tung kilns must be the same as those of Northern Kuan, since the latter also were traditionally located in a village south-east of the capital.[2] He suggests as possible examples of Tung, or Northern Kuan, two specimens in the Mukden Museum, one being an ewer also with deeply carved decoration and a pale bluish glaze and the other an unusual lobed bowl. How-ever, Koyama fully admits that such attributions are speculative and doubts whether satisfactory proof will ever be forthcoming: 'Due to repeated flooding of the Yellow River, K'ai-fêng was inundated again and again, so that the streets of the original Sung city lie buried deep below ground level. . . . Therefore, if the Northern Kuan kilns were actually in or near K'ai-fêng, their discovery would be little short of a miracle.'

Returning to the question of Northern Kuan, which has already been briefly considered in connection with official Ju ware, it is evi-dent that there are broadly three theories in the field. The first is that

---

[1] See Introduction to O.C.S. Catalogue cited in footnote 2 on p. 31, also Intro-duction to Section 1 of the *Illustrated Catalogue of the Percival David Foundation*, London, 1953.

[2] Dr. Chên states that the Northern Kuan kilns 'are said to have been in Chên-liu'—the very locality given in the *T'ao Lu* for the Tung factory. Kuo Pao Ch'ang held that Tung ware was made in Chên-liu, but Dr. Chên states: 'There are various theories about Tung ware, but we remain completely at a loss, since no kiln site has been found to the east of K'ai-fêng.'

---

(1) *Plate* 34; (2) *Plates 36 and 37*; (3) *Plate 35.*

Northern Kuan comprised a variety of wares made by highly skilled potters from different kilns who were brought to the capital for the purpose; the second that it was essentially Ju ware but may also have included pieces 'partly Chün and partly Ju in character', if not others of the class which has been called 'Kuan Chün'; and the third that it was a special type of ware made at the capital and probably derived from Tung, or else that it was Tung itself. There has long been in the British Museum a very lovely though much repaired bowl from the Alexander Collection (1) which Hobson originally described as coming nearest to his conception of Ju ware: 'The colour is precisely that of the most beautiful bluish green Corean bowls, but the usual Corean finish and the sand marks on the base are absent, and the glaze is broken by a large, irregular crackle.'[1] This was written long before Sir Percival David had identified Ju on the basis of a comprehensive study of the literary evidence supported by actual specimens in the Peking Palace Museum. Subsequently Hobson was content to refer to the bowl as a superior Sung ware, though differing from any of the known types, and to note that a Tung attribution had been suggested.[2] While clearly of northern provenance and datable to the early part of the Sung dynasty, this bowl presents a striking similarity in general form and structure to the fine Southern Kuan bowl in the Tokyo National Museum (2). We know from the T'ao Shuo that the Southern Kuan factory 'copied the porcelain formerly made at the old capital', and it would therefore not come as a surprise if the Alexander bowl proved to be a rare example of the earlier, Northern Kuan.

Whatever may have been its connection with Tung, Northern Celadon evidently was closely related to Yüeh ware—indeed, prior to the identification of the latter, most of the specimens in England and America were labelled Northern Celadon. It seems probable that some of the Yüeh potters migrated northward when the kilns fell on evil days, just as others may have crossed the sea and settled in southern Korea. The forms are often analogous and the carved designs not dissimilar. However, the Northern Celadon glaze is usually a dark olive-green with a somewhat frothy appearance, distinguishable from the pale green or olive of Yüeh ware, though a few beautiful specimens exhibit the tender green of growing plants and leaves. The finely incised decoration characteristic of Yüeh ware in the Five Dynasties or early Sung period also is not found in Northern Celadon, which relied more often on the use of moulds. The foot-rims, too, are generally

[1] R. L. Hobson, Chinese Pottery and Porcelain, Vol. 1, p. 59.
[2] R. L. Hobson, Handbook of the Pottery and Porcelain of the Far East . . . , p. 25.

(1) Plate 38; (2) Plate 54.

heavier and have 'burned' a deep brown or show a rough brownish gloss (1).

The discovery by Harada of Northern Celadon and Chün shards on the same sites has led Japanese experts to stress the affinity between these two wares. After noting a general similarity in body, shape and style, Koyama goes so far as to maintain that the ingredients of both glaze and body are almost identical, justifying his classification of Chün as a type of celadon. There is logic in this view, for the blue colour of most Chün ware is now known to be caused by iron fired in a reducing atmosphere like the varying green of celadon,[1] and the resemblance of one variety of Chün—Green Chün—to Northern Celadon has often been remarked. It is natural that there should be a family relationship between the two wares, for both seem to have been made at potteries in the same region; however, there are important divergencies, the most obvious being that Chün ware relies for its effect on colour, whereas Northern Celadon is distinguished by its carved decoration.

Northern Celadon is thus a direct descendant of Yüeh ware and a fairly close relative of Chün. Since methods and designs were freely copied by contemporary potters at different kilns, it will not be surprising that links have also been traced with other wares made at the same period—for example, the practice of combing detail and cutting radiating lines on the under-sides of bowls after the style of *ying-ch'ing* and the use of moulds for impressing patterns in the manner of Ting.

However, Northern Celadon differs from all other contemporary

[1] At one time Hobson believed that the blue colour of Chün ware was attributable to copper; the same view was held by Otani and, more recently, by Honey. However, it was rejected by Ozaki and other Japanese authorities and has been refuted by Hetherington (see the revised edition of *Chinese Ceramic Glazes*, South Pasadena, 1948, pp. 68–9). Koyama maintains that the Chün glaze differs from that of Northern Celadon solely as a result of straw-ash being used instead of wood-ash. It is worth quoting the views of a potter of great Far Eastern and other experience in this connection: in *A Potter's Book*, London, 1948, p. 241, Bernard Leach states that 'the old Chinese used to burn bracken and limestone together to make a flux for their porcelain glazes' and refers to 'the Yüan and Chün glazes in which rice-straw ash takes the place of bracken'. He continues: 'As in some celadons the bluish colour is due to a small percentage of iron in both glaze and body. It is a mistake to attribute the Chün blue to the presence of oxidized copper.' On the other hand, there is no doubt that the reddish or purple splashes often occurring in Chün ware have been caused by reduced copper, so that Dr. Chên, while agreeing with Koyama's classification of Chün ware as a type of celadon, notes that it commonly shows the effect of copper as well as iron, a feature which sets it apart from other wares regarded as celadon. On the relationship between Northern Celadon and Chün ware, Dr. Chên also supports the view propounded by Koyama that 'as a general rule the Northern Celadons are earlier and belong to the Northern Sung period, while the Chün wares are of the Southern Sung and Yüan'.

---

(1) *Compare Plates* 15, 16 *and* 47.

wares in the strongly individual character of its forms and in the depth and vigour of its carved decoration (1). Some of the jars and vases have strangely angular outlines (2), while the dishes and bowls show variant types of rim, turning inward at the edge or outward in a flattened roll (3). Whether carved, incised or moulded, the decoration is executed with sureness and vitality: the floral designs are well composed and normally cover the entire vessel or the inner surface of a dish or bowl. Often flying phoenixes are set against a background of floral scrolls (4), or ducks are seen swimming amidst waves; the design of boys playing among flowers also is not uncommon (5). In contrast to the originality displayed in the forms, the decoration tends to be conventional, yet the whole accomplishment is so masterly that it could only have been achieved by skilled craftsmen working to a tradition and on a grand scale.[1] It is hardly surprising that Japanese opinion has readily accepted the identification of Northern Celadon as Ju ware, for it would be difficult to point to any ceramic products which are more artistic or worthy of fame; yet it must be reaffirmed that we remain uncertain of the origin and identity of this beautiful class of ware.

$$\star \quad \star \quad \star \quad \star \quad \star$$

Since the above was written, word has come of a new discovery of great interest. Mr. Basil Gray, on his visit to China last summer, learned that a kiln site had been found very recently in Shensi province, west of Honan, where Northern Celadon wasters were excavated. It seems that these generally bore impressed or moulded decoration, and many examples of this kind in Western and Oriental collections are now thought to have been made at the Shensi factory.[2]

[1] It is clear from the number of surviving pieces that the volume of production must have been large, but Northern Celadon does not seem to have featured as an important export ware, probably for the reason suggested by Hobson, that it was made in the interior and far away from sea-ports engaged in overseas trade. However, it has been found along the overland route to Western Asia and in Chinese Turkestan on sites explored by Sir Aurel Stein, also at Fostât in Egypt and at Samarra on the River Tigris. A number of pieces have been excavated from Korean tombs, but not a single example has been found at sites in Japan.

[2] Mr. Basil Gray has kindly permitted publication of the following note: 'The kiln site for which I saw the evidence on my recent visit to China is 80 kilometres north of Sian, and the name given to me for the wares was Yao-yao. They told me that there is more than one kiln in Tung-chuan hsien; the other kilns are at Wang-pu, Shang-tien, Li-lu, and Ch'en-lu. Seggars, spurs and wasters have been found, and I saw one mould and also a bowl which had never been glazed. The commonest shape is a foliate bowl of lotus shape. I was told that the kiln had been active from the third century A.D. onwards, but, of course, the Celadon ware of the type we are concerned with is Sung.'

---

(1) *Plates* 39–52; (2) *Plates* 50A, 52A *and* B.
(3) *Plate* 45A; (4) *Plate* 51; (5) *Plate* 46B.

5

SOUTHERN KUAN

When the Sung Court fled southward from the invading Tartars and established a new capital at Hangchou, pottery kilns were set up in the vicinity of the Palace under the direction of an official named Shao. According to the *T'ao Shuo*, they were situated at the foot of Phoenix Hill and made a celadon (*ch'ing*) ware variously known as 'Palace ware' (*Nei yao*) and 'Official ware' (*Kuan yao*). They are said to have copied the porcelain made at the former capital, K'ai-fêng, and the best pieces were considered to be equal, or similar, to Ju ware.

It is often assumed that this development took place shortly after the transfer of the Court in 1127, but Baron Ozaki has pointed out that it is not likely to have occurred for several years, perhaps not until 1141, on account of the disturbed conditions which prevailed after the fall of K'ai-fêng. The former Emperor Hui Tsung, with most of his family and a large retinue, had fallen into the hands of the enemy, and it was one of his sons who was proclaimed Emperor, after escaping the general disaster and taking refuge at Nanking. Two years later the Tartars crossed the Yangtze and overran the provinces south of the river, capturing both Nanking and Hangchou. It was only after a long campaign that they were driven back northward by the reorganized Sung armies, and peace was not concluded until 1141.[1]

The practice initiated early in the century of establishing a special factory to supply the porcelain required by the Palace was thus continued under the Southern Sung. The original kilns were set up at the Hsiu-nei-ssu, which was the Imperial Household Department concerned with maintenance of the Palace buildings. Probably they were located in the area reserved for workshops and accordingly came under the same administrative management. It is usually held that they were in operation for only a short period, because the records state that new potteries were built later below Chiao-t'an, or the Altar of

---

[1] Dr. Moule gives details of the migration of the Court to the south—'a complicated series of wanderings which filled eleven years'—and notes that the *Sung Shih* ends by stating that the capital was not fixed at Hangchou until 1138 (A. C. Moule, *The Rulers of China: 221 B.C.–A.D. 1949*, London, 1957, p. 88).

Heaven, and that these also made official ware, though it was inferior to the earlier product. However, most Japanese authorities take the view that the Hsiu-nei-ssu kilns were active for some fifty or more years and may even have continued until the end of the dynasty.

Many attempts have been made to discover the sites of the Hsiu-nei-ssu kilns, but their exact location remains in doubt. It seems likely that they were later utilized for buildings to house the Palace staff or garrison, with the result that all trace of the kilns has been obliterated. In recent years further details have been given by Tsuneo Yonaiyama of his claim to have located the sites during a series of investigations carried out in the years 1928–30, but these have not added any convincing facts to his earlier account.[1] He states that he found altogether five kiln sites within or just outside the Palace grounds to the north-east of Phoenix Hill but admits that they were in a very confused and disorderly state as a result of subsequent building. Many fragments with white, black and various celadon glazes were collected by Yonaiyama besides others which are indisputably Kuan ware, and there are good grounds for the belief that these merely represented wares used by residents of the buildings. This was at all events the view taken by Hobson and other leading members of the Oriental Ceramic Society who visited the place in 1935, for they concluded that 'these were not factory sites but doubtless rubbish heaps of a district which had been covered with the villas of the well-to-do in Sung times'.[2] However, it cannot be said that Hobson's party made any very thorough investigations, whereas Yonaiyama insists that he found definite evidence of kilns in the form of saggars, stilts, shards fused together and other waste matter. He further maintains that several different kinds of ware, including one with a *ying-ch'ing* type glaze, were made at Hsiu-nei-ssu, though Kuan was of course the most important, and the fact that no reference to such a practice can be found in the literary records should perhaps not be regarded as conclusively disproving this theory. With regard to the Kuan ware made at Hsiu-nei-ssu, Yonaiyama holds that it is distinguishable from the later products of

[1] In *Shina Fudoki* (Chinese Customs), Kaijo-Sha Press, Tokyo, 1939. Yonaiyama states that he gradually came to realize the positions of the kilns as a result of living in the district and constantly searching for evidence: 'The only way of determining their location is to investigate the relics scattered about. The number of these would not amount to more than a few pieces in a year, or a few score in three years. Probably they could not be found by persons making only occasional visits to the district. There are many fragments of pottery scattered about, but in judging such relics we must bear in mind that this was the site of the Southern Sung Palace and that there were numerous subsidiary buildings round the main Palace as well as quarters for large numbers of troops.'
[2] R. L. Hobson, 'Notes on a Visit to Hangchow,' *O.C.S. Transactions*, Vol. 13, 1935–6, p. 36.

Chiao-t'an, having an almost white body and a pale bluish glaze not unlike that of *Kinuta* celadon and usually without crackle.

Probably the first Western visitor to the sites near Hangchou was Mr. Orvar Karlbeck, who has kindly supplied particulars of his investigations together with a transcript of notes made at the time of his trip in November 1932. One interesting point about this record is that it corroborates in several respects the claims made by Yonaiyama, which have never been published outside Japan and were unknown to Karlbeck himself. It seems that a Chinese investigator, Jên Chou, was among the first to explore the area and to find the site visited by Hobson's party as well as confirming the location of the Chiao-t'an kilns, to which reference will be made later. Karlbeck was taken to both places by Jên Chou, who was then Director of the National Institute of Engineering at Shanghai. He reports that the first site, located near the southern end of West Lake, had been much disturbed, not only by the building of the city wall during the Ming period but also by the construction of a wide road, which had taken place only a few years before his visit. This had probably destroyed any remains of kilns, and the only direct evidence was part of a saggar, which had been unearthed by Jên Chou during his previous investigations. Many shards, however, were collected in the vegetable fields beside the road, and these were broadly of two kinds. The first was 'remarkably like Lung-ch'üan', with a white porcelain body and a thick, even glaze of celadon type, mostly without crackle, while the second had a thinner, bluish white glaze like *ying-ch'ing*.

Referring to Hobson's later visit, Karlbeck notes that he sent full information concerning Jên Chou's researches and expresses surprise that little attention was paid to the tremendous upheaval caused by road construction or to the significant discovery of part of a saggar.[1] He is convinced that there were once kilns in the vicinity and rejects the view that the shards were all refuse from villas which may have been erected there subsequently.

Although the problem must remain unsolved until more thorough-going excavations have been carried out, there is no question that Yonaiyama's views have exercised considerable influence in Japan, where it is believed that some of the celadon fragments he collected were undoubtedly products of Hsiu-nei-ssu. Since most of these are remarkable for having an almost white body and a pale bluish glaze devoid of crackle, they have given rise to the theory that similar complete specimens of specially fine quality may be identified as Hsiu-nei-ssu ware. Certain examples of this kind in Japan and elsewhere seem

[1] Both points are, however, mentioned by Hobson in the David Catalogue, pp. xxiii–xxiv.

to be superior to Lung-ch'üan ware of the *Kinuta* class, which they closely resemble, and may be accepted as a type of Kuan.[1] But it is difficult to reconcile this attribution with literary references to the 'brown mouth and iron foot' and the 'crab's claw marking' which were said to be characteristic of Hsiu-nei-ssu ware and seem to indicate a porcelain with a darker body and some crackle. Indeed the weight of Chinese tradition supports the view that Southern Kuan was essentially dark-bodied and crackled, and later copies of Kuan are all of this type. Koyama recognizes this discrepancy but suggests that the records may have confused the earlier Hsiu-nei-ssu ware with products of the Chiao-t'an kilns, which have been reliably identified and correspond with the literary descriptions. In favour of this theory is a statement by a thirteenth-century writer that the new kiln ware of Chiao-t'an 'is already very different as compared with the old Kuan ware and the Nei ware'.[2]

[1] In his article: 'A Celadon Vase probably of Hsiu-nei-ssu Ware' in *Yamato Bunka*, No. 4, December 1951 (in Japanese) Koyama describes them as 'pale bluish and a grade higher in quality than ordinary *Kinuta* celadon: they have no crackle, their style is very refined, and I believe that there are no finer Chinese celadons in existence'. See Plates 60 and 61. Ozaki considers that their colour 'occupies an intermediate position between Ju yao and Lung-ch'üan yao' and that they 'exactly fit the description found in Sung sources concerning the earlier Southern Sung Kuan yao baked in the Hsiu-nei-ssu after the model of the Ju Kuan ware of the Northern Sung period' ('Chinese Literature on Ceramics,' *Oriental Art*, (New Series), Vol. III, No. 1, Spring 1957). The idea that there was a light-bodied Kuan ware is not new and may have been suggested originally by the *Liu Ch'ing Jih Cha* of 1573 (according to the version published as the *Liu Liu Ch'ing* and referred to in Sir Percival David's paper, 'A Commentary on Ju Ware,' *O.C.S. Transactions*, Vol. 14, 1936–7, p. 34 and Plate 14) which indicates that the body material was white, but this refers specifically to the type made in the north at K'ai-fêng before 1127. Kuo Pao Ch'ang maintained that Southern Kuan also was made sometimes 'by moulding white clay' (preface to Vol. II of the *Illustrated Catalogue of Chinese Government Exhibits* . . . , 1936, p. 17). Dr. Chên cites a passage from the *Ko Ku Yao Lun* (mentioned also in the *T'ao Shuo*—see p. 43 of Bushell's translation) which describes the earlier 'Palace ware' made at Hangchou and refers to dark-bodied porcelains of Kuan type known as *Wu-ni* (Black paste) ware and to imitations of these made at Lung-ch'üan; from this he infers that Hsiu-nei-ssu ware did not as a rule have a dark body and could thus be differentiated from copies made elsewhere. In the West the covered jar shown in Plate 59 was originally considered by Hobson to be Lung-ch'üan ware but is now regarded as Southern Kuan (*O.C.S. Exhibition of Ju and Kuan Wares*, Nov./Dec. 1952) and Sir Harry Garner considers that *Kinuta* celadon 'may have a colour indistinguishable from that of a Kuan piece of high quality' ('Ju and Kuan Wares of the Sung Dynasty,' *The Burlington Magazine*, Vol. XCIV, December 1952, p. 351). The tendency to regard specially fine celadons of this type as Kuan instead of Lung-ch'üan is thus not an exclusively Japanese development and warrants further study. Of course it is quite likely that skilled potters from Lung-ch'üan were employed at the Southern Kuan factories, just as Chün and other potters may have worked at the Northern Kuan.

[2] The *T'ao Lu* attributes this statement to Yeh Chih (see p. 62 of Sayer's translation) but probably as the result of an error in the *Cho Kêng Lu*; it seems likely to have been made by another thirteenth-century writer, Ku Wên-chien (see Sir Percival David, *op. cit.*, p. 28).

However, Koyama admits to certain doubts and agrees that a final solution must await the completion of further investigations at the Lung-ch'üan as well as at the Kuan sites.

In the West various specimens of Kuan porcelain have been suggested by Sir Percival David and other authorities as possible examples of Hsiu-nei-ssu ware but without much assurance, for it is generally believed that the only means of distinguishing the products of the earlier kilns from those of Chiao-t'an lies in their superior quality. This view is based on the Chinese literature, which makes no clear distinction between the two but indicates that it depended on the 'intrinsic workmanship'.[1] Since there is always some disagreement concerning the relative merits of individual specimens, it seems unlikely that any final conclusions will be reached on this basis. For the most part the records are content to describe the 'Palace ware' in general terms as a celadon (*ch'ing*) composed of fine material and exquisitely made: they praise its beautiful, translucent glaze and call it 'the delight of the age'. Such epithets could be reasonably applied to many existing specimens of Kuan but offer little ground for any attempt at discrimination.

The Western conception is thus in closer conformity with literary sources, but these have often proved an uncertain guide; the Japanese view rests on the evidence provided by actual field studies, the validity of which, however, is open to question.

The sites of the later kilns set up below Chiao-t'an, the Altar of Heaven, have been reliably located at the foot of Tortoise Hill, a southerly spur of Phoenix Hill. The remains of the Chiao-t'an factory were reported as long ago as 1913, but they do not seem to have attracted attention until 1929–30, when they were located by Jên Chou and investigated by Kōzui Otani and Tsuneo Yonaiyama. The whole area was found to be strewn with fragments and wasters and the remains of saggars. Since Yonaiyama's visit is the earliest of which full details have been published, it may be of interest to give a brief extract from his account:

'On the morning of February 26th 1930 I proceeded to the site, at first by car and then on foot. . . . On the slopes of the hill were scattered many pieces of saggars, also stilts with dishes and bowls still adhering to them and bricks melted by fierce heat. On the edge of some saggars bluish celadon glaze was adhering, melted from the porcelains. There could be no doubt that all these were relics of celadon kilns. They were scattered over a wide area. Calling a nearby farmer, I got him to dig here and there. I found then that the relics were only in a shallow

---

[1] *T'ao Shuo*, pp. 43–4 of Bushell's translation; this comment also is attributed to Yeh Chih—but see preceding footnote.

layer on the surface. Deeper excavation only exposed the red soil and revealed no trace of kiln debris. . . . I was told that many potsherds were to be found at a certain spot. On investigating the hollow pointed out to me, I observed countless fragments: they were all pieces of celadon ware with saggars and round stilts. It was without doubt an ancient kiln site. . . .

'I visited the locality several times to make further studies and collected many materials therefor. The number of fragments and kiln implements which I collected myself, noting the details, probably amounted to two or three thousand. I can state definitely that the sites of the "new kilns" are not in their original state but have been turned over repeatedly and the relics are all mixed up with sand and stones, etc. Such digging was caused by grave making in later times. Further, these were official kilns which made porcelain solely for the Imperial Household and their number was not large. They seem, too, to have been active for only a short period, so that it may be assumed the production was on a small scale. From this we can appreciate the true nature and significance of the Kuan kilns and their products.'

A few years later, in the early part of 1935, this site also was visited by Hobson and his party. The British Museum had already received some shards from Dr. Nakao, who expressed the view that the site was that of the Chiao-t'an factory. At the time, however, a different opinion was held by some Chinese authorities, and this may account for Hobson's statement in the David Catalogue that the site was actually that of Hsiu-nei-ssu. By the time he visited the locality all doubts had been dispelled, and he noted in a brief account of the trip that discovery of the site had enabled the later (Chiao-t'an) ware to be identified with certainty on the basis of the fragments recovered.[1]

Unfortunately there is a great deal of variation in the 'Altar Kuans', as they are often called. The body is normally grey but may be light coloured or so dark as to appear almost black. Frequently there is a blackish layer immediately next to the glaze, so that a fragment glazed on both sides and viewed in section shows a grey core sandwiched between black layers. There can be little doubt that this effect is attributable to the high iron content of the clay fired in a reducing atmosphere. Reference is often made to the 'black body' of the Altar Kuans —indeed Hobson notes that a stratum of black clay was observed in the vicinity of Chiao-t'an by Mr. Peter Boode—but it is probable that the original colour was pale brown and that the change to a darker tone took place during the firing.[2] Turning next to the glaze, this

[1] R. L. Hobson, op. cit., pp. 35–6.
[2] Bernard Leach states that a clay containing iron turns grey when reduced before the glaze over it has melted (A Potter's Book, London, 1948, p. 139). The un-

shows every variety of colour from light brown to bluish green or grey. The difference here also is attributable to the firing conditions and may be observed to some degree in all types of celadon, a bluish or greenish glaze being produced by reduction and brown by oxidation. However, it is clear that there was some variation in the material used for both body and glaze. Furthermore, there is the complication that Kuan ware is known to have been copied at other potteries. The Yü-hang kilns, some twenty-five miles north-west of Hangchou, made a similar ware and imitations also were made at Lung-ch'üan. Thus, we find many examples of Kuan type, sometimes described as 'Hangchou celadon', which cannot definitely be assigned to Chiao-t'an or to any other known kiln. If there is a type of Southern Kuan which comes very close to the *Kinuta* celadon of Lung-ch'üan (1), so also there are Chekiang celadons which approach the traditional and distinctive kind of Kuan, with a soft yet lustrous glaze and more or less crackle (2).

A number of excavated pieces and wasters, however, correspond so closely with the shards actually dug up at the kiln site that they must be accepted as authentic specimens of Chiao-t'an Kuan ware. Most of these are small vases, bowls and incense burners in many different shapes; often they are very thinly potted and have square or fluted sections which produce an effect curiously like that of metal. Nearly all show profuse crackle, often made more conspicuous by the greyish stain resulting from burial. It is characteristic of excavated pieces that the glaze shows much degeneration especially at the foot, where the several layers may be clearly marked and resemble the lines left on the shore by a receding tide (3). Many perfect specimens preserved in the Peking Palace and other collections also show close similarity to the shards and excavated pieces. They include vases of bronze form, bowls, dishes and incense burners (4).

Kuan ware is remarkable for the depth and quality of its glaze. Fragments from Chiao-t'an show that the glaze was applied in repeated layers and is often thicker than the body itself. This led Count Otani to propound an interesting theory that the Kuan kilns may have been established originally for the express purpose of producing an entirely new class of ware which combined very thin potting with an ab-

usually dark colour of the body is caused by the presence of an abnormally large amount of iron, five per cent as against less than one per cent in the usual porcelain body (Sir Harry Garner, *op. cit.*, p. 351).

---

(1) *Plates* 59, 60 *and* 61; (2) *Plate* 62.
(3) *Plate* 57B; (4) *Plates* 53–8 *and Colour Plate* C.

C. *Southern Kuan ware. Dish in the form of an eight-petalled flower*
covered with a translucent bluish glaze, widely crackled.
Sung dynasty. Diameter 6·7in.
Percival David Foundation. See page 46

normally thick and lustrous glaze.[1] Certainly Kuan ware is unique in
this respect, and the effect, whether brilliant and gem-like or subdued
as in polished marble, cannot be matched by any other type of porcelain. As already noted, the darkness of the body is caused by a relatively large amount of iron, while the opacity of the glaze is attributable to a high percentage of lime, fine particles of which are held in
suspension, as well as to countless minute bubbles.[2] The light reflected
by these suspended particles and bubbles produces a wonderfully
luminous tone.

It is necessary at this point to mention the confusing term *Ko*,
which originally referred to a special class of ware made, according to
the tradition, by the elder of the two Chang brothers at Lung-ch'üan.
A significant passage in the *T'ao Shuo* states that it was the presence of
crackle which distinguished the productions of the elder brother from
those of the younger, and the current view in the West is that the
term later came to be associated with crackle and to be applied generally to all types of ware in which this was a regular and conspicuous
feature. Most of the specimens which were formerly considered to be *Ko*
ware are not clearly distinguishable from Kuan and, on the new inter-
pretation, may be regarded as the variety of Kuan which has a close
and well-defined crackle and usually a whiter, more bubbled glaze.

A report has recently been published of researches carried out by
two American investigators on the sub-surface glaze structure of Kuan
ware.[3] Comparative studies were made of shards collected by Yonaiyama at Chiao-t'an together with complete specimens of Kuan ware
and some other wares, such as Yüeh and Northern Celadon. Micro-
scopic and other examination revealed a striking similarity in the
glaze, or more particularly in the structure of bubbles within the
glaze, of twelfth-century Kuan vessels and shards, whereas a marked

---

[1] Kōzui Otani, *Shina Kō-tōji* (Ancient Chinese Pottery), Tokyo, 1932, p. 53:
'Why were separate Kuan kilns established under the Northern Sung? It is said
that the Emperor Hui Tsung was a scholar and a skilled artist and that he con-
structed Kuan kilns at Pien-ching (the old name for K'ai-fêng) for the purpose of
making the wares he desired; however, this would have been unnecessary if he had
not wished to produce something which neither the Ting nor the Ju kilns could
make. . . . Ting ware is thinly potted and also has a thin glaze, while Ju ware has a
thick glaze and is thickly potted. Therefore the thing that neither of these kilns
could produce was a thick glaze like that of Ju on thinly potted ware like Ting. It
may have been that the Kuan kilns were originally established at Pien-ching in
order to make a ware combining these two features. . . . To judge from the Kuan
fragments from Chiao-t'an, the celadons of Pien-ching may well have had a thick
glaze applied over a thin body.'

[2] Sir Harry Garner, *op. cit.*

[3] Robert T. Paine, Jr. and William J. Young, 'A Preliminary Report on the Sub-
surface Structure of Glazes of Kuan and Kuan-type Wares,' *Far Eastern Ceramic
Bulletin*, Vol. 5, No. 3, September 1953.

contrast was noted in the eighteenth-century imitations bearing Ch'ien-lung and Yung-chêng reign-marks. The examples of Yüeh and Northern Celadon, though differing in certain respects from early Kuan ware, showed a general conformity in glaze structure and a similar divergence from the later Kuan copies. This led to the conclusion that the material used for both glaze and body in the twelfth century was coarsely ground and differed in composition from the finely prepared material in use during the eighteenth century. If these results are confirmed by further investigation, it would seem that an important advance has been made in the study of Chinese ceramic glazes and a means found for checking the date in doubtful cases. On the other hand, variations in glaze often occur on a single specimen and may be observed under ordinary magnification, so that it is too early to regard the tests as conclusive.

It has been thought that the Chiao-t'an potteries did not outlast the Sung dynasty, but attention has recently been called to a fairly well-defined group of Kuan wares which differ in some respects from the excavated pieces and shards and may have been made at a slightly later date.[1] The bodies are dark and the glaze an opaque and heavily crackled greyish white or brown. Many were fired on spurs, which is an unusual feature in excavated pieces; however, it occurs also on some authentic fragments, and a number of stilts with four or more spurs were collected at Chiao-t'an by Jên Chou and also by Yonaiyama. The quality and individuality of these wares differentiate them from the eighteenth-century copies, but their potting is somewhat thicker than that of most Chiao-t'an specimens and a late Sung or Yüan date has been suggested for the group as a whole, while a few are thought to have made as late as the Ming dynasty. It is, of course, quite possible that the Chiao-t'an potteries continued in operation after the Sung dynasty in a private or unofficial capacity; alternatively other local kilns may have continued to copy Chiao-t'an products after the original potteries had been abandoned.

It will be evident from what has been said that final conclusions on Kuan ware must await a thorough investigation of the kiln sites around Hangchou by trained archaeologists. Meanwhile, however, a great deal of material, some of which is without doubt trustworthy, has been accumulated and is available for further study by modern scientific methods. The literary records, as usual, are ambiguous, but it is worth mentioning one of the more reliable, the *Tsun Shêng Pa Chien*, written by Kao Lien in 1591, which formed the basis for the section on Kuan ware in the seventeenth century *Po Wu Yao Lun*, quoted later in the *T'ao Shuo*. Kao Lien refers specifically to the ware

[1] Sir Harry Garner, *op. cit.*

made at Hsiu-nei-ssu, but his description tallies with the fragments and wasters from Chiao-t'an and, if the Chinese tradition is to be trusted, may be regarded as appropriate to Southern Kuan in general. He states that the clay used was 'of brownish colour', which caused the foot-rim to assume an iron-coloured tone: 'People used to say of this ware: "Brown mouth and iron foot". The reason for the brown mouth is that the liquid glaze, being poured from above, ran down the side and covered the mouth less thickly than the rest of the vessel, so that at the mouth there were traces of the underlying brown. This is not in itself of any importance, but such points as the "iron foot" are valued because no other place possesses such valuable clay.' As to glaze colour, Kao Lien states that the pale bluish (*fên ch'ing*) is the best, followed by the thin white (*t'an po*) and the ash-coloured (*yu hui*). With regard to the forms, he considers that the imitations of ancient bronzes, of which a number have survived, 'constitute the first and most admirable class of Kuan pottery'.[1]

The main characteristics of Chiao-t'an Kuan ware have been usefully summarized by Koyama as follows:

'First, they have a specially large iron content—larger than that of any other ceramic ware. They are mostly coloured dark bluish grey, approaching black, but those which have been oxidized are grey-brown. Secondly, they have a porcelain body different from that of Lung-ch'üan ware and are therefore crackled over the entire surface: where the glaze is thick the crackle is heavy, and where it is thin the crackle is fine. A third point is that the wares are surprisingly thinly potted. . . . Especially in the case of the smaller dishes the glaze is often far thicker than the body—sometimes it is four or five times as thick, and sometimes the body is as thin as paper. The feet, ears and mouth-rims are delicately made and give an immediate impression that they are indeed the refined products of official kilns. . . . Fourthly, there is the glaze colour: at first sight it is close to the pale bluish of *Kinuta* celadon, but owing to the high iron content it has a deep, settled appearance. There are probably no other ceramic wares with such a smooth and lovely glaze. It has the charm of the sapphire and cannot fail to impress all who see it with its great beauty. However, not all specimens are equally fine: as stated in the *Tsun Shêng Pa Chien*, the majority are greyish due to insufficient reduction and others are the so-called loquat colour due to complete oxidation.'

[1] See translation by Arthur Waley in the *Year Book of Oriental Art*, London, 1925.

6

LUNG-CH'ÜAN WARE

By far the largest number of Chinese celadons were made during the latter part of the Sung period, through the Yüan and on into the Ming at extensive potteries near Lung-ch'üan in the southwestern corner of Chekiang province. Lung-ch'üan ware became so famous and the volume of production so great that the earlier celadon wares were eclipsed and almost lost to memory. In the West it gave rise to the very name of celadon and until recent years was considered easily the most important and beautiful of early Chinese porcelains.

Reference was made in the Introduction to the vast scale on which Lung-ch'üan ware was exported from China. Fragments have been found along all the trade routes in Central Asia, Persia, India, the East Indies, the Persian Gulf, Arabia, Egypt and down the African coast in Kenya and Tanganyika, while numerous complete specimens have been preserved in India, Egypt, Persia and Turkey, and even some in Europe. Shipments to Japan must also have been immense, to judge from the thousands of fragments collected on the beach at Kamakura as well as on the shores of Hakata Bay and at many historical sites in the interior. Indeed, the Japanese have always been enthusiastic admirers of Lung-ch'üan celadon, especially of the *Kinuta* vases and incense burners which were so highly esteemed by Tea-masters as ornaments for the *tokonoma*, or alcove for the display of works of art. A remarkable number of Lung-ch'üan vessels have been treasured in Japan from the time of their arrival many centuries ago; they are revered as *meibutsu* and *densei-hin*—celebrated art-objects and heirlooms handed down from former generations—and are regarded as part of the national heritage.

The Japanese cult of Lung-ch'üan celadon has given rise to descriptive terms, some of which have passed into world-wide use. Since these are liable to misinterpretation, some attempt at definition will not be out of place. Thus, celadon wares in general, and particularly Lung-ch'üan celadon, are divided into three broad groups, *Kinuta*, *Tenryūji* and *Shichikan*. The finest specimens, dating from the Sung period and exhibiting a beautiful bluish green glaze, have been called

Kinuta. This word means 'mallet' and is supposed to have been first applied to a particular mallet-shaped vase which possessed the admired blue-green tone. The vase in question is often assumed to be the one owned by Rikyū, the famous sixteenth-century Tea-master and arbiter of taste, which later passed into the ownership of Baron Iwasaki. This vase is adorned with handles or 'ears' in the form of fish and has a large crack along the side. Now the Japanese word *hibiki* has two meanings, signifying both a crack and the sound made by pounding clothes with a wooden mallet. The name *Kinuta* may thus have been derived from the shape of the vase or, by a play on words, from the crack which suggested the sound made by a mallet. Another claimant for the original name is a vase of similar shape but without any ears and therefore more truly in the form of a mallet; this vase has long been in the possession of the Tokugawa family, as the former Daimyōs of Kishu. There are other claimants besides the two just mentioned, and the *Kinuta* vase which nowadays receives the highest praise is no doubt the superb example owned by the Bishamon-dō Temple in Kyoto (1). However, the feature which all the vases hold in common is an ethereal bluish green glaze colour, and the term *Kinuta* has thus come to be generally applied to Lung-ch'üan celadons of this type regardless of their shape. In China the colour is known as *fên ch'ing*, or pale bluish green. Japanese descriptions refer eloquently to the 'graceful forms and dripping blue-green glaze' of *Kinuta* wares.

The term *Tenryūji* is derived from an incense burner with relief peony decoration preserved at the temple of that name in Kyoto and refers to Lung-ch'üan celadon of the Yüan and early Ming period which had assumed a faintly yellowish green tone. There is a variant theory as to the derivation, attributing it to ships of that name which brought the wares to Japan in the fifteenth or sixteenth century. Hobson described *Tenryūji* celadon as 'a fine sea-green', but this is not in strict accord with the Japanese conception, though it is necessary to tread warily when seeking to draw such a fine distinction. A pale olive tinge may be regarded as characteristic of the *Tenryūji* class of Lung-ch'üan ware, and the description 'pea-green'—also used by Hobson in some cases—would perhaps be more appropriate.

Finally we come to the *Shichikan* type, reputedly brought from China by an official of the seventh (*shichi*) grade. This refers to Lung-ch'üan ware dating from about the middle of the Ming period, when a further change in the colour and tone of the glaze became apparent. *Shichikan* celadon is characterized by a transparent, almost watery green glaze, sometimes with a hint of blue, through which the body

---

(1) *Plate* 66.

can often be clearly seen. Since a bluish or alternatively an olive tone depended on the firing conditions, which were always variable, it is difficult to regard colour alone as a valid criterion, and Koyama admits that 'there are numerous gradations between *Kinuta*, *Tenryūji* and *Shichikan* which can hardly be described in words'. Perhaps the chief distinction is rather one of quality, and there is significance in the fact to which this grouping draws attention that a progressive decline took place from the *Kinuta* celadon of Southern Sung to the *Tenryūji* of Yüan and early Ming and finally to the coarse and superficial *Shichikan* of the middle Ming and later. Though somewhat arbitrary and based on aesthetic rather than scientific grounds, it is the only qualitative differentiation which has been attempted and seems now to correspond broadly with the dynastic periods in which the wares were made.

According to the legend repeated many times in Chinese literary sources, there were two brothers of the Chang family, Shêng-i and Shêng-êrh, who each had a pottery in the Lung-ch'üan district.[1] The elder Chang is said to have made a special class of ware known as *Ko*, but we have seen in the chapter on Southern Kuan that this name has led to much confusion, being used later to describe various crackled wares and especially the crackled variety of Kuan. For this reason it is now thought by many Western scholars that the term became virtually synonymous with crackle and lost its original precise significance. Koyama does not go quite so far as this but suspects that 'Ming connoisseurs confused *Ko* with Kuan ware and their error has been perpetuated to the present day'. The identity of the original *Ko* ware is not made any clearer by these subsequent mistakes or changes in usage.

The *T'ao Shuo* maintains that it was the presence of crackle which distinguished the productions of the elder brother from those of the younger, and there seem to be good grounds for believing that the earlier variety of Lung-ch'üan was essentially a crackled ware. Sir Percival David has suggested that this was in all probability the type of celadon made near Lung-ch'üan during the Northern Sung period, while the Court was still at K'ai-fêng, and that it may have approximated to the peasant pottery class.[2] Dr. Chên agrees that *Ko* ware was characterized by crackle, which was either wide and irregular or close-meshed, and varied in colour from bluish green to brown; but he

---

[1] See page 47. The Chang brothers seem to have been active in the Southern Sung period. Hobson quotes a late source, the K'ang Hsi Encyclopaedia *Ch'in Ting Ku Chin T'u Shu Chi Ch'êng*, as indicating their continuance into the Yüan period, but this must be regarded as doubtful. Koyama states that the local annals of Lung-ch'üan hsien make no attempt to give the exact dates of their lives.

[2] Sir Percival David, Introduction to *O.C.S. Catalogue of an Exhibition of Ju and Kuan Wares*, reprinted in *O.C.S. Transactions*, Vol. 27, 1951–3.

makes no claim to have obtained satisfactory evidence from the kiln sites. He links this early crackled celadon with the Lung-ch'üan copies of Southern Kuan, of which important finds were made in 1939, but admits that there is nothing to indicate whether the latter were made by the elder brother; they would in any case be datable to the Southern Sung period.[1]

We are on firmer ground when we come to consider the products of the younger Chang, who is said to have 'improved upon the output of his elder brother in the fineness of his work and the excellence of his designs'.[2] One reason for this, as suggested by Sir Percival David, may well have been the arrival of the Court at Hangchou and its subsequent support and patronage. Abundant kiln site evidence supports the tradition that the smooth, uncrackled celadon of Lung-ch'üan, mainly dating from the Southern Sung period, was the class of ware which the younger Chang raised to world-wide fame.

According to tradition, Lung-ch'üan ware of this type was first made in the Northern Sung period, but no proof of this has yet been obtained. Probably it was preceded by such varieties, also made in Chekiang, as the 'scraped base ware', which we have tentatively assigned to Li-shui (pages 23–4), and the 'grey ware', which is so close to Yüeh but is certainly a transitional type (page 19). Koyama points to the more archaic funerary jars and vases with dragons or tigers in relief curling round the shoulders (1) (Dr. Chên states that these were made as pairs, one having a tiger and the other a dragon) or with several spouts projecting upwards as likely to have been made in the Northern Sung, when such

[1] In his section on Lung-ch'üan ware, after a brief discussion of the *Ko* type, Dr. Chên writes: 'There are also copies of the Southern Sung Kuan wares of Chiao-t'an which resemble the latter so closely in colour and finish that, according to some writers, it is difficult to distinguish between them; but it is not known whether these copies of Kuan wares were made by Chang Shêng-i or not. It was in 1939 that fragments and complete pieces of this kind were discovered, i.e. at the time when China was at war with Japan, near Tayao and at Yut'ou in Lung-ch'üan hsien. These pieces were found twenty feet below the surface of the ground. Their body was black and many were very thin, those from Yut'ou being far superior to the others. It had been thought that the crackled wares (of Lung-ch'üan) were of heavier make, but this idea was seen to be incorrect. . . . The glaze was very fine and had been thickly applied.' There is an extraordinary waster in the Metropolitan Museum of Art, New York, consisting of two bowls which have become fused together in the firing. One of the pair seems to be an ordinary Lung-ch'üan celadon with a light-coloured body, while the other is a dark-bodied ware of Kuan type with profuse crackle. Possibly the latter represents the class described by Dr. Chên, but it is difficult to account for the two pieces being fired together. Could this have been the normal practice at the kilns concerned or was it merely accidental?

[2] According to the *Ch'ing Pi Tsang*, published in 1595, quoted in the *T'ao Shuo.*

(1) *Plate* 64.

shapes are thought to have been popular. Dr. Chên also believes that these are among the earliest of the Lung-ch'üan products. When we come to the Southern Sung period, however, the amount of material recovered from the kiln sites—though largely undocumented—becomes quite bewildering.

Excavation of the Lung-ch'üan kiln sites has proceeded for many years. Koyama states that large-scale digging took place in 1916–17, when 'crowds of art-dealers from Shanghai, Hangchou and elsewhere thronged to the area.' Enterprising Chinese speculators purchased large plots of land on which there were heaps of kiln refuse and systematically excavated all the fragments and wasters within their territory. Not until 1928 was any serious investigation carried out: in that year Dr. Chên visited the locality and collected a great deal of material. In 1934 he paid a second visit, and summary reports of his discoveries were published in the following year.[1] A brief survey has also appeared in Dr. Chên's recent historical sketch of Chinese celadon wares (see Bibliography). No other important studies of the Lung-ch'üan sites seem to have been published, and the area has by this time been so much disturbed that it may well prove difficult to unearth further data of any significance, except where this lies deeply buried.

Dr. Chên exhibits the true bent of the scholar by decrying the collector's preoccupation with perfect specimens and preferring 'odds and ends discovered at the kiln sites as material for study'. His time at Lung-ch'üan was thus fruitfully employed, though he was able to examine only a limited number of the two hundred or more kiln sites which have been located. The most important of these were at a place called Tayao, where 'the whole area was littered with debris and waste saggars, enabling one to collect as many specimens as desired'. Over a score of inscriptions, mostly in seal-characters, were found on fragments at Tayao, and Dr. Chên regards this factory as pre-eminent, all the shards being of the highest quality and including many of the *Kinuta* class. He believes that this was the original pottery of the younger Chang, though it is impossible to determine at which of the thirty-six kilns so far located he actually worked. It was surmised that transportation from Tayao must have presented difficulty, for the place is a mountain village and it must have been necessary for the output of the kilns to be carried by porters or mules. It was therefore natural as production increased for the kilns to spread eastward along either side of the River Tach'i, whence rafts could be floated downstream, and there was evidence that such a development had taken place. Furthermore, the Tayao kilns had clearly continued in operation well into the Ming period, for a large number of the fragments—including

[1] In *Tōji*, Vol. VII, No. 5, October 1935.

most of those with inscriptions—were of Ming type and some bore the name *Kushih*, which is thought to refer to the potter Ku-shih-chêng, active about the Chêng T'ung era (1436–49).

Since it must have taken some considerable time for the fine glaze and technique perfected by the Chang brothers to be developed, Dr. Chên felt sure that there was an earlier type of Lung-ch'üan celadon, but he was unable to find any traces of this. According to the *T'ao Shuo*, the brothers Chang worked at Liu-t'ien, and this has been identified as the original name by which Tayao was known. There is a tradition that the kilns were finally destroyed by flood, and Dr. Chên found definite signs that 'they had all been abandoned simultaneously as a result of some misfortune'. The *T'ao Lu* remarks that the kilns were moved from the Lung-ch'üan to the Ch'u-chou district, near Li-shui, at the beginning of the Ming period, but this is evidently a too sweeping statement and there seems to be insufficient justification for the practice of describing later celadons of Lung-ch'üan type as 'Ch'u-chou ware', although the *Ko Ku Yao Lun* states that this name was sometimes used in early Ming times. We do not know enough about the course of events, but it is clear from the shards collected near Lung-ch'üan that a large part of the industry must have remained in the vicinity well into the Ming period. The current practice of calling heavily crackled specimens 'Hangchou ware' likewise has little in its favour: many different types of celadon have been picked up at Hang-chou, but there is no real evidence of kilns in that neighbourhood, apart from those of the Southern Kuan ware discussed in the preceding chapter. It seems on the whole preferable to retain the designation 'Lung-ch'üan ware' in all cases except where another locality is specifically named in an inscription or where the class of ware differs materially from the Lung-ch'üan type and seems likely to have been made in another part of Chekiang province. In this connection it should be noted that there is considerable variation in the shards collected at different kiln sites near Lung-ch'üan, so that what we have termed the 'Lung-ch'üan type' must be understood to cover a much wider field than would normally be the case.

Tayao is situated about twenty-five miles southwest of the town Lung-ch'üan. Other kiln sites have been located at Chuk'ou and Fêngt'ang, some miles to the west, the products of which are characterized by heavy potting and thick glaze. Lower down the River Tach'i towards Lung-ch'üan are many more kiln sites, one of the most important being at Tama. The fragments collected at this place were of fine quality and clearly dated from the Sung period. Nearby lay the hamlet Ch'ik'ou, where Dr. Chên chanced on a specimen he describes as '*Ko* ware—covered with fish-roe crackle'. 'It may be', he adds, 'that

Tama was the location of the *Ko* kilns'—but time did not permit him to make a more thorough investigation.

Lung-ch'üan ware was mass-produced, yet the profusion of different shapes allowed full scope for the potters' creative talent. Among the more successful and therefore abundant forms are conical bowls or flat dishes of various sizes with lotus-petal carving outside (1), dishes or basins with a pair of fishes or a dragon moulded in relief inside (2), incense burners of cylindrical or tripod shape (3) and many different kinds of vase besides the mallet-shaped *Kinuta*, not a few of which were clearly copies of archaic bronzes (4). Although some of the pieces thus have carved or moulded designs, their simplicity and purity of shape and the absence of elaborate decoration stand out in contrast to many earlier wares including Northern Celadon and Yüeh and seem to reflect the new conception of classical refinement at the Sung Court, of which the official wares, Ju and Kuan, were the archetypes. So vast was the production of every kind of vessel that a certain impression of standardization is almost unavoidable; yet the workmanship and quality of the glaze seem to achieve uniform excellence. Variations occur chiefly in the tone or colour, and the Chinese, who use the word *ch'ing* indiscriminately to describe any kind of blue or green, delight in such subtle distinctions as 'onion-green' and 'cucumber-green', the true significance of which is difficult to grasp and impossible to describe. There are in any case few more lovely sights in the whole field of ceramic art than a group of Lung-ch'üan celadons, with their smooth, soft glaze texture and restful tints ranging from the heavenly blue-green of the *Kinuta* through the vivid grass-green and jade-green to olive-green and dove-grey. As in Southern Kuan ware, the soft effect is caused by the presence of hosts of minute bubbles and small particles of unmelted matter which are held suspended in the glaze and reflect light in all directions. When these impurities are absent, the glaze is transparent and the underlying body clearly visible. This is often the case with the later Lung-ch'üan ware of the Ming dynasty; probably it was the result of a higher temperature being employed in the firing, causing the air bubbles to disperse and the fusible material to become completely incorporated.

The body of Lung-ch'üan ware is greyish white in colour but has turned reddish brown wherever it was unprotected by a covering of glaze; often there is a red-brown fringe where the glaze comes to an end at the foot. The reason for this change of colour is that the body is highly ferruginous, and it is often said to have 'burned red in the

---

(1) *Plate* 74A *and* B; (2) *Plate* 77; (3) *Plates* 65B, 67 *and* 69.
(4) *Plate* 72.

D. *Mallet-shaped vase with phoenix handles. Lung-ch'üan ware*
(*Kinuta type*).
Sung dynasty. Height 11 in.
Fitzwilliam Museum, Cambridge. See page 56

firing.' As remarked by Hetherington, it would be more accurate to say that the body has 'turned red in the cooling', for the change of colour has taken place at the end of the firing process, when the air is freely admitted into the kiln. Previous to this, a strongly reducing atmosphere has been produced by use of a smoky flame; carbon monoxide has formed and has captured as much as possible of the available oxygen. The bluish green tone of Lung-ch'üan celadon is thus primarily attributable to the smoky firing which has converted the small amount of iron present into ferrous oxide. But when the kiln is swept out with fresh air at the end of the firing, the aerial oxygen reacts on the hot exposed body where it is not protected by glaze and converts the iron in it to reddish ferric oxide. The oxygen has no effect on the glaze at this time but only on the body where it is exposed at the foot-rim or elsewhere.

This characteristic of the clay used in making Lung-ch'üan ware led to an ingenious method of stressing the decoration by contrasted colours: the potters moulded fishes or dragons inside their dishes and deliberately left these designs bare of glaze, with the result that they turned a rich brown and stood out strikingly against their green background (1). Another very attractive though more subdued effect is seen where the 'ribs' of a carved or moulded form show lighter through their thin glaze covering (2). A type of Lung-ch'üan ware much favoured in Japan is the *tobi seiji*, or 'spotted celadon', distinguished by spots or splashes of dark brown which were produced by drops of ferric oxide on the celadon glaze (3). It seems that these two-colour effects were introduced toward the end of the Sung dynasty and came into vogue in the Yüan and early Ming. Later, copper-red was sometimes used in splashes or designs under the celadon glaze. However, preoccupation with decorative features usually seems to be accompanied by a decline in other qualities, and only the earlier examples retain the elegance of form and delicate *Kinuta* glaze which are the hall-marks of Sung Lung-ch'üan ware.

It is interesting to note that one of the best-known Lung-ch'üan vessels is expressly mentioned in the *Ko Ku Yao Lun*: 'there is one kind of dish on the bottom of which is a pair of fishes, and metal rings are attached as handles.' Many such dishes have survived of all sizes, and some have holes pierced in their rims for handles. In a few cases the metal handles themselves have remained. Another type is represented by two fine dishes in the David Foundation bearing stamped

---

(1) *Plates 79B and 83*; (2) *Plates 71 and 72*.
(3) *Plates 76 and 85A*.

square seals with the characters *ho pin i fan*:[1] these refer to the story of a legendary Emperor who once made pottery on a river-bank. The same inscription occurs on a Lung-ch'üan bowl excavated from a tomb in Korea, and it is worth noting that all three pieces are decorated with radiating lines drawn in white slip under the glaze. Fragments also were collected by Dr. Chên at the Tayao kiln sites and by Dr. Nakao at Hangchou with the same square seal mark.

Koyama attributes the decline in the quality of Lung-ch'üan ware to increased popularity and consequent enlargement of output, both for domestic use and for export overseas: 'As exports increased year by year, more and more kilns were established around Lung-ch'üan; as a natural result the competition grew keener and brought about an increase in the number of roughly-made wares, while the raw material became poorer and the style and technique deteriorated. . . . Improved methods of production led to increased variety in the shapes and enlargement of the size of individual pieces, but this accentuated a tendency to rely on inferior materials.' There is no definite evidence to support these views, but they may be considered valid deductions from the trend shown by dated specimens; it seems very probable that the supply of high-grade material was restricted or even that deposits of the best clay finally became exhausted. The changes in quality certainly did not take place suddenly, so that here must have been periods of overlapping and the inferior glaze material which produced the olive-toned *Tenryūji* class no doubt came into use while *Kinuta* celadon was still being made at the leading kilns. The demand for Lung-ch'üan ware, however, evidently reached such proportions toward the end of the Sung period that maintenance of the former high standards must have become difficult and a certain deterioration therefrom almost inevitable.

Dr. Chên was at pains to discover the source of the clay used in making Lung-ch'üan ware and mentions twenty different places where it was mined, all of which he visited for the purpose of collecting specimens. An abundant supply of raw material was thus clearly available within easy range of the potteries, but the fact that so many deposits were utilized indicates the magnitude of the industry and suggests that considerable variation in the products might be expected. This may help to explain the wide diversity noted earlier as a feature of the shards collected at the kiln sites and evident also in complete specimens of the ware.

Some further details may be of interest concerning the extraordinary number of Lung-ch'üan fragments—mostly of Sung date—which have been collected on the beach at Kamakura, the seat of

[1] David Catalogue, Plate XXXVII.

government in Japan from the end of the twelfth to the middle of the fifteenth century. Koyama estimates the total at about fifty thousand, or far more than have been recovered from any other place excepting the kiln sites themselves. Various theories have been put forward to account for this phenomenon. Kamakura was a large and populous city in the thirteenth century and after, and it is possible that the fragments were carried down to the sea by rivers or floods from the rubbish-heaps on which broken vessels were thrown, or alternatively they may have come from junks laden with celadon wares which were sunk by storms off the coast. The most likely theory is that they are the remains of porcelains found to be damaged after the voyage from China and therefore thrown overboard while the ships were unloading. Similar finds have been made at Hakata Bay on the southern island of Kyushu, and a Japanese writer has pointed out that they show some differences when compared with fragments excavated from historical sites inland: 'they are generally larger and their surface is less worn; this leads us to suppose that wares found broken after the voyage were thrown into the sea while the ships were anchored in port and have lain buried in the sea-bed ever since.'[1] Koyama quotes a contemporary record which refers to hundreds of ships anchored off Yuigahama, the sea-shore and former port of Kamakura, and there is plenty of evidence that trade and intercourse between China and Japan grew very rapidly, especially after the Sung Court removed to Hangchou. Records are preserved of the visits made to China by some seventy or eighty Japanese Buddhist priests and abbots during this period, and it is worth noting that many fragments of *Kinuta* celadon, as well as some complete specimens, have been recovered from the sites of temples and shrines in the Kamakura region. Similar relics also have been unearthed at the sites of large residences, and it seems that the wares must have been in general use in prosperous households. In exchange for the vast quantities of porcelain imported from China the Japanese exported such commodities as gold, sulphur, swords, fans and timber. Interesting discoveries continue to be made at Kamakura: within the last few years a pair of unusually large and fine conical bowls of Sung period Lung-ch'üan ware were dug up by a gardener: probably these had been buried for safety several centuries ago and never subsequently recovered.

In modern times Japanese potters have excelled at making copies of Sung Lung-ch'üan ware, and some Chinese reproductions, though less well known, are equally skilful. Imitations of *Kinuta* vases are regularly offered for sale at department-stores in Tokyo, where they com-

[1] Heijiro Nakayama in an article on ancient Hakata in the Japanese journal *Kōkogaku Zasshi*, Vol. XVI, No. 9.

mand high prices and are used as tea-room ornaments in middle-class households. The fact that such pieces continue to be fashionable reflects the esteem in which Sung celadon is held in Japan. However, despite their excellent glaze and finish, they have a somewhat 'machine-made' appearance and would hardly deceive any experienced person. On a much higher plane are some truly remarkable copies made by leading Japanese potters which often show as much character and individuality as the authentic—though mass-produced—originals. In many cases these will baffle the most expert, and no easy means to recognition can be offered. The problem is to detect a subtle difference between productions which achieved rare beauty despite the technical limitations of their time and present-day copies made by potters of equal skill who accepted the same disabilities as an artifice. A well-known story tells how the manager of a world-famous Japanese art-dealer acquired in America a superb *Kinuta* vase and relates his discomfiture on suddenly realizing in mid-Pacific that the piece was one of a series commissioned by his own firm from a noted Kyoto potter. With such an occurrence in mind, it will be appreciated that no distinctive criteria of such wares can be put into words. The existence of some obvious blemish might lead to the conclusion that a specimen is one of the many genuine wasters which have been excavated from the kiln sites and put on sale; but even this is not a sure guide, for at least one Japanese potter is said to have made deliberate copies of these—spoiled by some ingeniously contrived 'mishap' in the firing.

7

CELADON OF THE YÜAN
AND MING PERIODS

While certain changes took place in the character of Lung-ch'üan celadon from about the end of the Sung dynasty, it is often a matter of difficulty to distinguish between the Sung and the Yüan or early Ming wares. Shape, style and glaze continue to be the chief criteria. Since the Lung-ch'üan and other celadon kilns in southern Chekiang were in no sense official factories, they were unaffected by the change of dynasty, and the fact that a large proportion of their output was exported acted as a stimulus to increased production, while possibly contributing to the gradual lowering of standards.

The type of celadon ware made in the Yüan and early Ming period has become clearer with the discovery of dated specimens, several of which may be seen at the David Foundation. Probably the most important is a large vase of baluster shape with a flaring, trumpet mouth, decorated with a bold peony scroll in relief and bearing an inscription round the lip (1). This states that the vessel was made by potters of the Liu (probably short for Liu-hua) hill near Liu-t'ien (or Tayao) in the Lung-ch'üan district and gives a date corresponding to 1327. Both the style and glaze colour of this fine vase are of the kind known to the Japanese as *Tenryūji* from an example preserved at a temple in Kyoto. Similar specimens have been treasured by temples in many parts of Japan and were once thought to date from the Ming period, but it is now clear that the change from *Kinuta* to *Tenryūji* celadon took place earlier, proably about the end of the Sung dynasty. It has been suggested that the *Kinuta* class may not have outlasted the Sung period, but there is no definite evidence either way. Further changes in the style of vases are indicated by two other examples also in the David Foundation which bear inscriptions with the dates 1432 and 1454 (2). A dish in the Tokyo National Museum is incised with the characters *Ta Ming Hsüan Tê Lung-ch'üan*, and a bulb-bowl formerly in the

---

(1) *Plate* 82; (2) *Plates* 88 *and* 90.

Eumorfopoulos Collection also bears a Hsüan Tê reign-mark, indicating manufacture during the years 1426 to 1435.

The tendency toward increased size and thickness mentioned by Koyama is very noticeable in some of the Yüan and early Ming celadons. Indeed it has become doubtful whether a Sung attribution is any longer tenable in the case of relatively large vases and dishes. Whether this development was influenced by the growing export trade to the Middle East is an open question, but there is no doubt that the strength and durability of these imposing pieces helped to ensure their survival. In the Topkapu Palace at Istanbul there are some 1,300 celadons mainly of this type, probably the most important group remaining in existence. A systematic study of this collection should go some way toward clearing up many obscure questions of dating. According to a brief but informative description by Mr. John Pope,[1] most of the pieces are large, heavily potted vases and dishes, and a number of the vases are similar to the famous specimen in the David Foundation mentioned above which bears the date 1327; no doubt these may be assigned with confidence to the fourteenth century, regardless of the exact technique employed in producing their vigorous relief decoration.[2] Some of the vases seem to have had their bases made separately and fused on to the upper parts when they were fired in the kilns. The large dishes and bowls exhibit two standard types of base, some being glazed all over except for a large ring up to an inch in width between the foot-rim and the centre, which was left in the biscuit and turned red-brown during the firing,[3] while others have an unglazed foot-rim and a recessed area in the centre of their fully-glazed base. The decorative patterns, often moulded in relief and reserved in reddish biscuit against the celadon green, include flowers and fishes and dragons among clouds, the latter sometimes having biscuit rosettes spaced round the rim (1). Since many of the carved and incised designs duplicate those

[1] John Alexander Pope, *Fourteenth-Century Blue-and-White: A Group of Chinese Porcelains in the Topkapu Sarayi Müzesi, Istanbul*, Washington, 1952, pp. 18–19.

[2] Some specimens, like the vase in the David Foundation, have had the surface carved away to leave floral scrolls in relief, while other examples have had floral scrolls applied in relief to the surface, but it cannot be maintained on the basis of the pieces so far known that the two techniques represent any significant difference in date.

[3] Probably this effect was intensified by the application of some ferruginous material, as suggested by John Ayers in 'Some Characteristic Wares of the Yüan Dynasty,' *O.C.S. Transactions*, Vol. 29, 1954–5, p. 73; he also points out that the techniques of glazed and biscuit reliefs were evidently interchangeable, since the dragon decoration on both types sometimes came from an identical mould—see Plates 83 and 86.

(1) *Plate* 83.

on blue-and-white wares of the fifteenth century, it is reasonable to suppose that these were executed at about the same time, or in the early part of the Ming period. In his recent survey of the porcelains formerly preserved in the Ardebil Shrine, near the Caspian Sea, but now removed to Teheran, Mr. Pope again draws attention to some close parallels between the decorative *motifs* found on the blue-and-white and celadon wares.[1] Since a great deal more study has been given to blue-and-white than to the later celadons, the chronology established for the former may be reasonably applied to the latter wherever there is striking similarity in the shapes or decorative designs, and in most cases it seems that a fourteenth or early fifteenth century date would be appropriate. Perhaps it is not too optimistic to expect that considerable progress in dating will result from further critical analysis of these relationships between the two classes of ware.

Thus, it is too early to attempt any precise dating of the celadons made from about the end of the Sung dynasty to the early Ming. The specimens bearing inscriptions may generally be regarded as reliable landmarks, but few of these have survived and the stylistic and decorative indications which may serve as a guide to dating the rest have not yet been fully worked out. In general it seems that many examples which were formerly considered to be Sung may well be Yüan or Ming. Thus, Mr. Schuyler Cammann has drawn attention to certain dragon-like *motifs* appearing on a number of celadon platters usually about fourteen inches in diameter.[2] These have been regarded as Sung wares, chiefly because the celadon glaze is of good quality and has a bluish tone, while the design of a strongly moulded dragon pursuing a sacred pearl within a border of vaguely incised floral scrolls presents the grace and simplicity of the earlier period (1). However, Mr. Cammann believes that the creature portrayed is actually a *tou-niu*, distinguished by downward-curving horns and a jewel-bearing tail, and that the platters so decorated are likely to be Ming, because this mythical beast does not seem to have been used for decoration—or perhaps invented—until the Ming period.

Among the thirty-two kiln sites listed by Dr. Chên in the Lungch'üan district, twelve are believed to date from the Sung period, six of these continuing on into the Ming, while fourteen more were established in the Yüan and Ming, the remaining six being of Ch'ing

[1] John Alexander Pope, *Chinese Porcelains from the Ardebil Shrine*, Washington, 1956, pp. 153–8.
[2] Schuyler Cammann, 'Some Strange Ming Beasts,' *Oriental Art* (New Series), Vol. II, No. 3, Autumn 1956, pp. 99–100.

(1) *Plate* 89.

date. Most of the fragments bearing inscriptions which were collected at Tayao also are thought to date from the Ming period. While this survey is not claimed to be anything like complete, it indicates the expansion of the industry at Lung-ch'üan during the Yüan and Ming periods, when some twenty of the kilns were in operation as against twelve in the Sung. But there is general agreement in the Chinese literature that the products of the kilns were not to be compared with those made earlier: the *Tsun Shêng Pa Chien* of 1591 states that they were strong and thickly potted but not as beautiful as before, and some were 'barely fit for use'. Koyama states that the same criticism is made in the local annals of Lung-ch'üan hsien.

During this time, however, exports probably reached their zenith. A large number of Ming celadons have been preserved in Japan as well as in the Middle East, and they became very popular for use in the Tea Ceremony, despite their relatively poor quality. Koyama refers disparagingly to a celadon vase in the Nezu Collection as 'a very poor, dull specimen' but adds: 'the choice of such an ordinary vase which seems to have no special merit is perhaps the keynote of our Tea Ceremony.' He suspects that the *Tenryūji* celadons which became so much admired as Tea Ceremony wares may date from the middle Ming, when the further change to the *Shichikan* type was about to take place.

By the second half of the fourteenth century increased competition was developing from the great pottery centre of Ching-tê-chên, where the production of white porcelain decorated in underglaze blue had reached large proportions. The large dishes and vases of celadon ware seem to have fallen into disfavour and to have been replaced by similar blue-and-white pieces. *Shichikan* celadons thus largely consist of smaller vases, incense boxes, desk ornaments and ink pallets, often of elaborate design. Even more complicated are the rock shrines, usually in two or three storeys, occupied by the figures of sages and their attendants modelled in the round; probably these were made throughout the Ming period—one of the best-known examples bears an inscription dated 1406.[1]

Koyama states that he has been unable to trace any definite evidence on the final stages of the industry at Lung-ch'üan, but the local annals indicate that few of the kilns survived into the late Ming: 'The reason for the decline is said to be the mass-production of poor quality wares and the rise in popularity of the blue-and-white and red-enamelled wares of Ching-tê-chên. Natural calamities also may have affected the kilns—for example there is a tradition that the Tayao kilns were destroyed by flood, while most of the settlements in the

[1] See *O.C.S. Transactions*, Vol. 8, 1928–30, p. 12 and Plate V. This class of ware is thought to have been made in Kwangtung province rather than in Chekiang.

Chuk'ou region perished at the hands of invaders. In a short while the prosperous Lung-ch'üan potteries had declined to poor rural kilns producing miscellaneous wares. The clay and glaze material, however, was not subject to such vicissitudes and continued to be available after these disasters: to this day there are kilns in operation in the Lung-ch'üan district, but their output is restricted to such things as roof-tiles, drain-pipes, braziers and water-pots.'

In addition to making the blue-and-white porcelain for which they became so famous, the potters of Ching-tê-chên also tried their hand at the production of celadon. Dr. Chên states that celadon ware had been made in this locality as far back as the T'ang period, but it was superseded by the bluish white *ying-ch'ing* during the Sung; however, 'with the unprecedented expansion of the industry at Ching-tê-chên in the Ming period many copies of the celebrated Sung celadons were made and not a few of these have survived to this day.' He cites a vase in the Peking Museum which has a soft, bluish green glaze and is believed to date from the Yung Lo era (1403–24): 'the colour of this vase rivals that of the most beautiful products of Lung-ch'üan—indeed the Lung-ch'üan kilns of that time were no longer able to produce such fine celadon of bluish green tone.' Copies of Ju, Kuan and *Ko* also were made, and the small vases with ears and small hexagonal cups made in *Ko* style during the Ch'êng Hua era (1465–87) are said to be quite common. Increasing archaism led to the wholesale copying of early celadon wares at Ching-tê-chên during the Ch'ing period, but it seems that this practice began earlier than had been thought.

8

THE CH'ING CELADONS

Relatively little significance is nowadays attached by Chinese and Japanese scholars to the Ch'ing celadons. Interest in these later productions also has waned in the West, and it is not difficult to understand the change in viewpoint from former times. For the earlier celadon wares all show strong individuality, and to this their form, style, body, glaze and even decorative designs make a definite contribution; but when we consider the Ch'ing celadons, we are compelled to admit that their attractive colouring and graceful shapes do not make up for the loss of more profound qualities: it seems that the original inspiration has given place to mere technical proficiency, with the result that a certain weakness or superficiality has become apparent. For all their skill, versatility and genius for imitation, the Ch'ing potters fell far short of the achievements of Sung and Yüan, and celadon became only one of many different glazes applied as a rule to a pure white and somewhat lifeless porcelain body. Koyama maintains that no celadon ware of importance was produced after the Yüan period: 'There are some pieces with a beautiful glaze and refined style among the Ching-tê-chên celadons of the early Ch'ing period, but careful examination reveals that these are but copies of the early wares, lacking their depth, mystery and spiritual power.'

The typical celadon glaze of the early Ch'ing period is a fine, transparent olive-green or 'sea-green', through which the white body is clearly visible, lightening the tone of the green. Specimens with a clair-de-lune glaze sometimes recall the pale bluish tint of the *Kinuta* celadons and Kuan ware. Ch'ing monochromes were seldom left quite plain, and it is usual for the celadons to have engraved decoration, such as dragons, under the glaze (1), or sometimes designs in white slip. The celadon glaze was not used solely as a monochrome, but also was applied locally in combination with underglaze red and blue decoration, the underglaze red often appearing at its best when covered with a pale celadon glaze. The use of reign-marks in underglaze blue,

---

(1) *Plate* 94.

found also on some Ming celadons, adds a somewhat incongruous note. All celadon wares were held in great esteem by French connoisseurs of the eighteenth century, and many fine Ch'ing celadons are still found with elaborate ormolu mounts added by European artists of that period.

Reference was made in the preceding chapter to the copies of Ju, Kuan and *Ko*, as well as to those of Lung-ch'üan ware, which were made at Ching-tê-chên from the Ming period onward. This archaism greatly increased in the Yung Chêng (1723–35) and Ch'ien Lung (1736–95) eras (1). Under the direction of the celebrated T'ang Yin the official factory at Ching-tê-chên reproduced with astonishing *expertise* every variety of glaze and surface texture, so that the Emperor Ch'ien Lung in later years mistook copies for originals, intensifying a confusion which has persisted into modern times. To this day the owners of perfect specimens of Kuan and other wares can never be quite free from the misgiving that some cherished example may, after all, be no more than an ingenious eighteenth-century imitation, for no infallible method of distinguishing between the two has yet been found. Dr. Chên states that the copies made at this time are superior to those made in the Ming period: 'the brown mouth and iron foot effect is so fine that virtually no difference can be detected from the Sung wares.' Where scholarship is thus at a loss, reliance can only be placed on the ability of the connoisseur to discern the creative power which invests an original production, its 'soul', and to sense the weakness or false value which must be inherent in an imitation.

The celebrated record of Père d'Entrecolles, who visited the Ching-tê-chên potteries early in the eighteenth century, contains the following account of some ingenious artifices adopted at the time for imitating the early wares and producing subtle effects to baffle collectors:

'The mandarin of King-tê-chên, who honors me with his friendship, makes to his patrons at the imperial court presents of old porcelain, which he has the talent of making himself. I mean that he has discovered the art of imitating ancient porcelain, or at least that of medium antiquity; he employs at this work a number of artisans. The material of which these false *ku-t'ung*—that is ancient counterfeits— are made is a yellowish clay, which is brought from a place not far from King-tê-chên, called Ma-an-shan (Saddle-back Hill). They are very thick; a plate of this kind which the mandarin gave me weighs as much as ten ordinary plates. There is nothing peculiar in the workmanship of this kind of porcelain, except that it is given a glaze prepared from a yellow rock, which is mixed with the ordinary glaze, the latter predominating; this mixture gives to the porcelain a sea-green

---

(1) *Plates* 95B *and* 96A.

colour. After it has been baked it is immersed in a very strong bouillon made of fowls and other meat; it is stewed in this a while, and is afterward put into the most filthy sewer that can be found, where it is left a month or more. When it comes out of this sewer it passes for being three or four centuries old, or at least for a specimen of the preceding dynasty of the Ming, when porcelain of this colour and thickness was highly esteemed at court. These false antiques are also similar to the genuine things in that they do not ring when struck, and emit no humming vibrations when held close to the ear.'

(Translation by Bushell in *Oriental Ceramic Art*, New York, 1899, p. 357.)

SHORT BIBLIOGRAPHY

IN ENGLISH

S. W. Bushell, *Description of Chinese Pottery and Porcelain, being a translation of the T'ao Shuo.* Oxford, 1910.

Basil Gray, *Early Chinese Pottery and Porcelain.* London, 1953.

R. L. Hobson, *Chinese Pottery and Porcelain,* 2 vols. London, 1915.
Chinese Pottery and Porcelain in the Collection of Sir Percival David. London, 1934 (referred to as David Catalogue).
Handbook of the Pottery and Porcelain of the Far East preserved in the Department of Oriental Antiquities, British Museum. 2nd edition, 1937.

W. B. Honey, *The Ceramic Art of China and other countries of the Far East.* London, 1945.

G. R. Sayer, *Ching-tê-Chên T'ao Lu, or the Potteries of China.* London, 1949.

The Chinese Exhibition: a commemorative catalogue of the International Exhibition of Chinese Art, Royal Academy of Arts, Nov. 1935–March 1936. London, 1936.

Arte Cinese—Chinese Art: Exhibition of Chinese Art. Venice, 1954.

Transactions of the Oriental Ceramic Society, London. From 1921.

Far Eastern Ceramic Bulletin. From 1948.

Oriental Art. From 1948.

IN JAPANESE

Fujio Koyama, *Shina Seiji Shi-ko* (A History of Chinese Celadon). Tokyo, 1943. (All quotations from Koyama are taken from this work except where otherwise indicated in footnotes.)

Tōji (Oriental Ceramics), 1927–43.

Tōsetsu (Journal of the Japan Ceramic Society). From 1953.

CHINESE CELADON WARES

In Chinese

Wan-li Chên, *Chung Kuo Ch'ing Tz'u Shih Lue* (History of Chinese Celadon). Peking, 1956. (All quotations from Dr. Chên are taken from this work except where otherwise indicated in footnotes.)

Wen Wu T'san K'ao Tzu Liao (Journal of Museums and Relics).

INDEX

INDEX

Lindberg, Gustaf, xvii
Li-shui ware, 23–4, 53

Matsumura, Yuzō, 9–12, 16, 18
Moule, Bishop, 19
Moule, Dr. A. C., 40
Mukden Museum, 36

Nakao, Dr. Manzō, 4, 15, 17, 28, 45, 58
Newton, Dr. Isaac, 23
New York Metropolitan Museum of Art, 15, 53
Nezu Collection, 64
Ninnaji Temple, 20
Northern Kuan ware, 30–2, 36–7, 43

Otani, Count Kōzui, 25, 27–9, 30, 38, 44, 46–7
Oxidation, xv–xvi, xvii, 2–3, 46, 56–7
Ozaki, Baron Junsei (or Nobumori), 4, 29, 30, 31, 32, 38, 40, 43

Palmgren, Nils, 35
Paine, Robert T., 29, 47–8
Peking Palace Collection, 34, 37, 46, 65
Pi-sê yao (or ware), xvii, 4, 5, 14, 17, 18, 19, 25, 26, 29
Phoenix Hill, see Hsiu-nei-ssu
Plumer, James Marshall, 14, 15, 20
Pope, John, 62–3

Reduction, xvii, 2–3, 45–6, 56–7

Samarra, 20, 39
Sarre, Dr. Friedrich, 20
'Scraped base ware', see Li-shui ware
Shang-lin-hu, 4, 12, 13–20
Shichikan class, 50–2, 64
Stein, Sir Aurel, 39

Tayao, 53, 54–5, 58, 61, 64
Tê-ch'ing, 7–9
Tenryūji class, 50–1, 58, 61, 64
Ting ware, 30, 33, 34, 38, 47
Tobi seiji, 57
Tokyo National Museum, 37, 61
Topkapu Palace, xvi, 62
Tung ware, 31–2, 35–7

Umehara, Dr. Sueji, 6

Waley, Arthur, 49
'Warham bowl', xvi

Yamato Bunka Kan Collection, 19
Ying-ch'ing ware, 27, 34, 38, 42, 65
Yo-chou ware, 23
Yonaiyama, Tsuneo (or Yasuo), 7–9, 15–16, 41–2, 44–5, 48
Yoneda, Shigehiro, 14
Young, William J, 47–8
Yü-wang-miao, 14
Yü-yao, see Shang-lin-hu

THE PLATES

1. *Tripod vessel of bronze shape with winged handles
and animal-mask finial decorated with impressed rope-bands
and spirals under a mottled olive glaze.
Precursor of Yüeh ware. Period of Warring States. Ht. 6 in.
Museum of Eastern Art, Oxford (Ingram Collection). See page 3*

2A. *Tripod vessel of bronze shape decorated with stamped spirals under a mottled olive glaze. Precursor of Yüeh ware. Period of Warring States. Ht. 5¼ in. See page 3*

2B. *Three-legged kettle with animal spout and fins, similar decoration and glaze. Precursor of Yüeh ware. Period of Warring States. Ht. 7¾ in. Museum of Eastern Art, Oxford (Ingram Collection). See page 3*

3A. *Small jar with moulded decoration of diamond diaper, flowers and equestrian masks. Yüeh ware, probably made at Chiu-yen. Han dynasty. Ht. 4 in. See pages* 7, 11, 13

3B. *Basin on three legs in the form of animal heads with moulded diamond diaper and t'ao-t'ieh masks. Yüeh ware, probably made at Chiu-yen. Han dynasty. Diam. 8 in.*

Museum of Eastern Art, Oxford (Ingram Collection). See pages 7, 11, 13

4A. *Dish with incised wave pattern and moulded design of animals and flowers. Yüeh ware. Han dynasty. Diam. 7 in.*
Lord Cunliffe. See page 7

4B. *Water-pot or brush-washer in the form of a toad holding a wine-cup to its mouth. Yüeh ware. Han dynasty. Length 5·9 in.*
Mrs. Walter Sedgwick. See pages 7, 11

5. *Basin with incised decoration of two fishes inside and moulded
diamond diaper and t'ao-t'ieh masks outside.
Yüeh ware, probably made at Chiu-yen. Han dynasty. Diam.* 12¾ *in.
Percival David Foundation. See pages* 7, 13

6A. *Bear-lamp. Yüeh ware, probably made at Chiu-yen.*
Late Han or Six Dynasties. Ht. 4½ in.
Percival David Foundation. See pages 7, 13
6B. *Sheep-pen. Yüeh ware, probably made at Chiu-yen.*
Late Han or Six Dynasties. Width 4⅜ in.
Museum of Eastern Art, Oxford. (Ingram Collection). See page 13

7A. *Model of a ram. Yüeh ware. Six Dynasties. Length 6 in.*
Sir Alan Barlow. See page 13

7B. *Lion-candlestick (or water-vessel). Yüeh ware, probably made at*
Chiu-yen. Six Dynasties. Length 5 in.
Lord Cunliffe. See page 13

8A. *Flask with loops for sling and moulded* t'ao-t'ieh *masks. Yüeh ware.*
Six Dynasties. Ht. 8¾ in.
Museum of Fine Arts, Boston (Hoyt Collection). See page 13
8B. *Ewer with 'chicken-head' spout. Yüeh ware, probably made at*
Tê-ch'ing. Six Dynasties. Ht. 10½ in.
Japanese collection. See page 9

9. *Ewer with 'chicken-head' spout. Yüeh ware. Six Dynasties. Ht. 18½ in. Hakone Art Museum (Japan). See page* 9

10A. *Vase with flaring mouth of square shape, curling at the edge and scalloped. Yüeh ware, probably made at Shang-lin-hu. T'ang dynasty.*
Ht. 4⅜ in.
Museum of Eastern Art, Oxford (Ingram Collection). See page 16
10B. *Box in lotus form with petals carved in relief on the cover.*
Yüeh ware, probably made at Shang-lin-hu. T'ang dynasty. Ht. 4⅜ in.
Fitzwilliam Museum, Cambridge. See page 16

11A. *Foliate cup. Yüeh ware, probably made at Shang-lin-hu.*
T'ang dynasty. Diam. 3·8 in. See page 16
11B. *Round pot with lotus-petal carving outside. Yüeh ware,*
probably made at Shang-lin-hu. T'ang dynasty. Ht. 3 in.
Museum of Eastern Art, Oxford (Ingram Collection). See page 16

12. *Ewer with incised decoration of parrots inside medallions.*
Yüeh ware, probably made at Shang-lin-hu.
Five Dynasties or early Sung. Ht. 5·7 in.
Courtesy of the Metropolitan Museum of Art, New York.
See page 17

13. *Ewer excavated at Kobata, near Kyoto. Yüeh ware, probably made at Shang-lin-hu. Five Dynasties or early Sung. Ht. 8·54 in. Kyoto Museum (Japan). See page* 20

14. *Box with incised design of a* cash *containing four characters surrounded by floral scrolls. Yüeh ware, probably made at Shang-lin-hu. Five Dynasties or early Sung. Diam.* 4⅞ *in. Percival David Foundation. See page* 17

15. *Dish with incised design of two phoenixes, the outside carved with overlapping lotus-petals; on the base is the incised character* yung *(eternal). Yüeh ware, probably made at Shang-lin-hu.*
Five Dynasties or early Sung. Diam. 6·9 in.
Percival David Foundation. See page 17

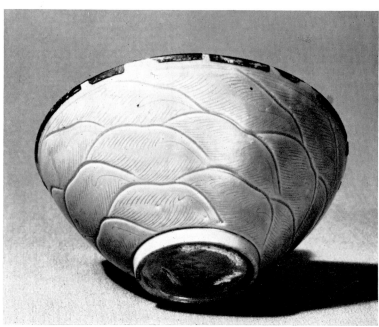

16. *Bowl with carved and incised design of the heads of two dragons emerging from waves in pursuit of a 'pearl', a rim of base gold round the mouth. Yüeh ware, probably made at Shang-lin-hu. Five Dynasties or early Sung. Diam. 5·7 in. Percival David Foundation. See page 17*

17. *Bowl with carved decoration of dragons among waves. Yüeh ware, probably made at Shang-lin-hu. Five Dynasties or early Sung. Diam. 10·8 in.*
Courtesy of the Metropolitan Museum of Art, New York. See pages 15, 17

18A. *Box with moulded decoration of boy playing among flowers.*
Yüeh ware. Five Dynasties or early Sung. Diam. $4\frac{1}{8}$ *in.*
Museum of Eastern Art (Ingram Collection). See page 17
18B. *Box with carved peony decoration. Yüeh ware.*
Five Dynasties or early Sung. Diam. $5\frac{7}{16}$ *in.*
Courtesy of the Smithsonian Institution,
Freer Gallery of Art, Washington. See page 17

19. *Jar with ovoid body and small mouth, decorated with boldly carved petal band; four loop handles on the shoulder. 'Grey ware' of Yüeh type. Five Dynasties or early Sung. Ht. 9 in.*
Museum of Eastern Art, Oxford (Ingram Collection). See page 19

20. *Covered vase with loop handles and carved floral decoration, a crinkled band of applied relief round the shoulder. 'Grey ware' of Yüeh type. Five Dynasties or early Sung. Ht. 12⅜ in. Museum of Eastern Art, Oxford (Ingram Collection). See page 19*

21. *Ewer with loop handles. 'Grey ware' of Yüeh type.*
Five Dynasties or early Sung. Ht. 8 in.
Museum of Eastern Art, Oxford (Ingram Collection). See page 19

22. *Covered vase with loop handles and incised inscription dated 3rd year of the Yüan Fêng period* (A.D. 1080). *'Grey ware' of Yüeh type.*
Sung dynasty. Ht. 14·8 *in.*
Percival David Foundation. See page 19

23A. *Bowl with engraved lotus-petal decoration under a pale olive-green glaze. Possibly Hung-chou ware. T'ang dynasty. Diam. 6 in.*
Sir Alan Barlow. See page 22

23B. *Water-pot on three small feet with a soft, bluish-green glaze. Unknown ware. T'ang dynasty. Ht. 4½ in.*
Museum of Eastern Art, Oxford (Ingram Collection). See page 22

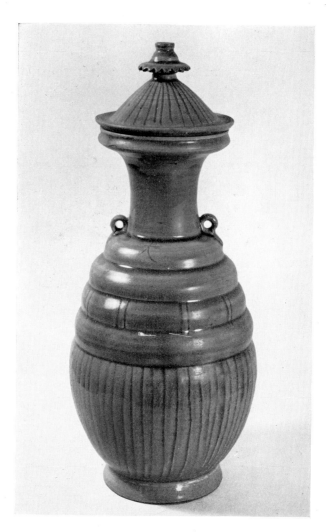

24. *Covered vase with loop handles and incised lines, inscribed with the*
character Ta *('Great'). Possibly Li-shui ware.*
Five Dynasties or early Sung. Ht. 8¾ in.
Museum of Eastern Art, Oxford (Ingram Collection). See page 23

25. *Vase with flaring mouth and carved petal decoration.
Possibly Li-shui ware. Five Dynasties or early Sung. Ht. 4·7 in.
Museum of Eastern Art, Oxford (Ingram Collection). See page 23*

26. *Vase (mei-p'ing) with carved decoration of floral scrolls above overlapping petals. Possibly Li-shui ware. Early Sung.*
Ht. 10·6 in.
Museum of Eastern Art, Oxford (Ingram Collection). See page 23

27. *Ewer with carved floral decoration and loop in flower form on either side of the neck. Possibly Li-shui ware. Early Sung.*
Ht. 6¼ in.
Sir Alan Barlow. See page 23

28A. *Ritual disc with incised inscription dated 1st year of the Ta-kuan era (1107). Ju ware. Sung dynasty. Diam. 3½ in. See page 30*
28B. *Dish. Ju ware. Sung dynasty. Diam. 5·9 in.*
Percival David Foundation. See page 35

29. *Vase. Ju ware. Sung dynasty. Ht.* 9·75 *in.*
Percival David Foundation. See page 35

30. *Stand for bowl with lobed saucer rim carved in the form of overlapping petals. Ju ware. Sung dynasty. Diam.* $6\frac{1}{2}$ *in.*
Sir Harry Garner. See page 35

31. *Dish with six faintly indicated lobes and foliate edge. Ju ware.*
Sung dynasty. Diam. 5¼ in.
Mrs. Alfred Clark. See page 35

32. *Bowl. Ju ware. Sung dynasty. Diam. 6·6 in.*
Percival David Foundation. See page 35

33. *Shallow dish. Ju ware. Sung dynasty. Diam. 6·9 in.*
Mr. Yasunari Kawabata. See page 30

34. *Ewer with soft bluish green glaze over a greyish body.*
Possibly Tung ware. Sung dynasty. Ht. 7·3 in.
Japanese Collection. See page 36

35. *Ewer with strongly carved floral decoration*
under a pale green glaze.
Possibly Tung ware. Sung dynasty. Ht. 8½ in.
Lord Cunliffe. See page 36

36. *Ewer with deeply carved floral decoration and spout in the form of
a seated lion. Possibly Tung ware. Sung dynasty.*
Ht. 7⅜ in.
The Cleveland Museum of Art (J. H. Wade Collection). See page 36

37. *Carved decoration on handle of ewer (see Plate 36)*

38. *Bowl with six faintly indicated lobes and foliate edge, grey body and soft bluish green glaze with some crazing; very thinly potted. Unknown ware, possibly Northern Kuan or Tung. Sung dynasty. Diam. 9½ in. British Museum. See page 37*

39. *Wine pot in animal form on three feet, decorated with carved phoenixes and peony scrolls, the handle surmounted by a human figure. Northern Celadon ware. Sung dynasty. Ht. (with handle) 8¼ in. Courtesy of the Metropolitan Museum of Art, New York. See page 39*

40. *Bottle with carved floral decoration. Northern Celadon.*
Sung dynasty. Ht. 9·4 in.
Victoria and Albert Museum. See page 39

41. *Lobed bowl with carved peony decoration. Northern Celadon.*
Sung dynasty. Diam. $5\frac{3}{4}$ in.
Mrs. Walter Sedgwick. See page 39

42. *Ewer with carved peony decoration excavated in Korea.*
Northern Celadon. Sung dynasty. Ht. 11·4 in.
National Museum, Tokyo. See page 39

43. *Lobed bowl with carved peony decoration excavated in Korea.*
Northern Celadon. Sung dynasty. Diam. 5·9 in.
National Museum, Tokyo. See page 39

44. *Bowl with carved lotus-petal design outside. Northern Celadon.*
Sung dynasty. Diam. 5¾ in.
City Art Gallery, Bristol. See page 39

45A. *Shallow dish with rounded everted lip and carved peony decoration.*
Northern Celadon. Sung dynasty. Diam. $7\frac{1}{2}$ *in. See page* 39
45B. *Small bowl with fluted sides. Northern Celadon. Sung dynasty.*
Diam. 4·7 *in.*
Fitzwilliam Museum, Cambridge. See page 39

46A. *Shallow dish with moulded peony decoration. Northern Celadon.*
Sung dynasty. Diam. 6¾ in.
Mrs. Alfred Clark. See page 39
46B. *Bowl with moulded decoration of boys playing among flowers.*
Northern Celadon. Sung dynasty. Diam. 6 in.
Courtesy of the Metropolitan Museum of Art, New York. See page 39

47. *Reverse view of bowl shown in Colour Plate A. Northern Celadon.*
Sung dynasty. Diam. 9½ *in.*
Capt. Dugald Malcolm. See page 38

48A. *Sprinkler carved with design of peonies and lotus-petals.*
Northern Celadon. Sung dynasty. Ht. 8·6 in. See page 39
48B. *Ceremonial bowl and stand; inside the bowl are nine dragon heads*
modelled round a reticulated dome; carved peony arabesques decorate
the exterior of the bowl and top part of the stand, the five legs being
carved into masks. Northern Celadon. Sung dynasty.
Ht. (bowl) 3·6 in. (stand) 4·9 in.
Museum of Fine Arts, Boston (Hoyt Collection). See page 39

49. *Incense burner or stand for bowl. Northern Celadon. Sung dynasty.*
Ht. 7½ in.
Mrs. Walter Sedgwick. See page 39

50A. *Vase with carved peony decoration. Northern Celadon.*
Sung dynasty. Ht. 6½ in.
Baron Iwasaki. See page 39
50B. *Box with carved peony decoration. Northern Celadon.*
Sung dynasty. Diam. 7 in.
Percival David Foundation. See page 39

51. *Pillow with carved decoration of flying phoenix and peonies.
Northern Celadon. Sung dynasty. Length $9\frac{1}{4}$ in. Width $7\frac{3}{4}$ in.
Baron Iwasaki. See page* 39

52A. *Vase with carved floral scrolls. Northern Celadon.*
Sung dynasty. Ht. 4⅖ *in.*
Mr. Kodaira. See page 39
52B. *Incense burner on three legs with carved floral decoration.*
Northern Celadon. Sung dynasty. Ht. 4⅖ *in.*
National Museum, Tokyo. See page 39

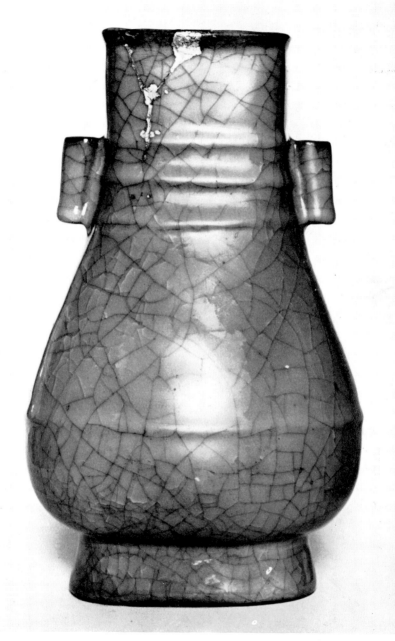

53. *Vase with tubular handles and heavily crackled grey-blue glaze.*
Southern Kuan ware. Sung dynasty. Ht. 10 in.
Mrs. Alfred Clark. See page 46

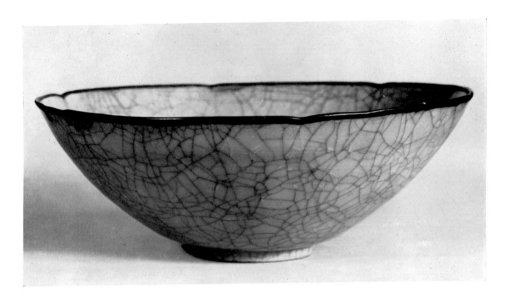

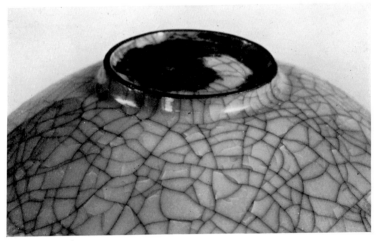

54. *Bowl with foliate edge and lustrous, bluish green glaze, heavily crackled. Southern Kuan ware. Sung dynasty. Diam. 10 in. National Museum, Tokyo. See pages 37, 46*

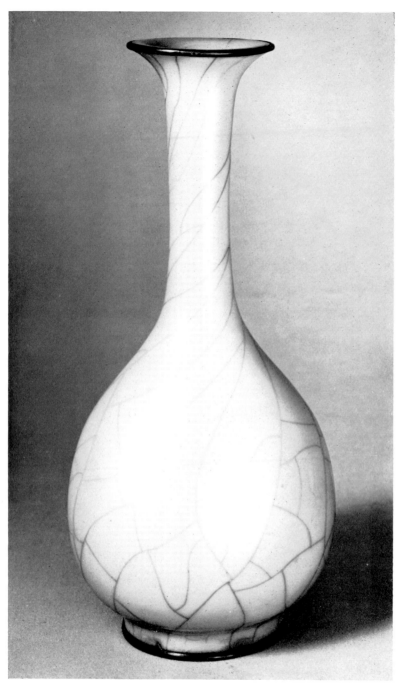

55. *Vase with lustrous, pale bluish glaze and wide irregular crackle.*
Southern Kuan ware. Sung dynasty. Ht. 7·1 in.
Percival David Foundation. See page 46

56A. *Conical bowl with lustrous, bluish green glaze, widely crackled.*
Southern Kuan ware. Sung dynasty. Diam. 6 in.
Sir Alan Barlow. See page 46
56B. *Lobed dish with lustrous grey-blue glaze, widely crackled.*
Southern Kuan ware. Sung dynasty. Diam. 7½ in.
Sir Harry Garner. See page 46

57A. *Vase with crackled grey-blue glaze supported on a thin circular foot. Southern Kuan ware. Sung dynasty. Ht. 5¼ in.*
Sir Alan Barlow. See page 46

57B. *Jar with crackled grey-green glaze, showing decomposition from burial. Southern Kuan ware. Sung dynasty. Diam. 5 in.*
Museum of Eastern Art, Oxford (Ingram Collection). See page 46

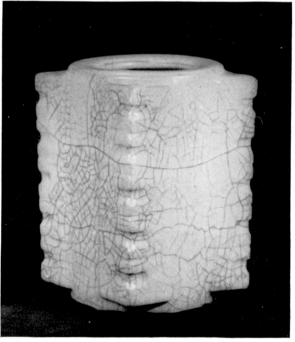

58A. *Incense burner on three legs with lustrous, bluish green glaze,*
heavily crackled. Southern Kuan ware. Sung dynasty. Diam. 5 in.
Baron Iwasaki. See page 46

58B. *Vase in the form of a jade ritual vessel with heavily crackled,*
bluish grey glaze. Southern Kuan ware. Sung dynasty. Ht. 7¾ in.
National Museum, Tokyo. See page 46

59. *Ribbed jar with foliate cover and pale lavender-blue glaze.*
Southern Kuan ware. Sung dynasty. Height 5 in.
Mrs. Alfred Clark. See pages 43, 46

60. *Mallet-shaped vase with pale bluish glaze. Southern Kuan ware* (?).
Sung dynasty. Ht. 9·9 *in.*
Mr. Hikotaro Umezawa. See pages 43, 46

61. *Dish with pale bluish glaze. Southern Kuan ware* (?). *Sung dynasty.*
Diam. $6\frac{3}{4}$ *in.*
Hakone Art Museum (*Japan*). *See pages* 43, 46

62. *Octagonal vase with soft but lustrous green glaze and wide crackle.*
Chekiang celadon of Kuan type. Sung dynasty. Ht. $8\frac{1}{4}$ *in.*
Sir Alan Barlow. See page 46

63. *Vase with incised decoration of lotus scrolls and overlapping petals
under a very pale green glaze. Chekiang celadon.
Sung dynasty. Ht. 9¾ in.
Mrs. Alfred Clark. See page 55*

64. *Funeral vase with cover surmounted by a dog, a coiling dragon in full relief round the neck; on the base is incised the character Ti ('Earth'). Lung-ch'üan ware (Kinuta type). Sung dynasty.*
Ht. 10⅛ in.
Mrs. Alfred Clark. See page 53

65A. *Vase in bamboo style. Lung-ch'üan ware (Kinuta type).*
Sung dynasty. Ht. 11¾ in.
Nezu Museum, Tokyo. See page 56
65B. *Incense burner. Lung-ch'üan ware (Kinuta type).*
Sung dynasty. Diam. 6¼ in.
National Museum, Tokyo. See page 56

66. *Mallet-shaped vase with phoenix handles. Lung-ch'üan ware
(Kinuta type). Sung dynasty. Ht.* 12·1 *in.
Bishamon-dō Temple, Kyoto. See page* 51

67. *Incense burner on three legs. Lung-ch'üan ware (Kinuta type).*
Sung dynasty. Diam. 5·5 in.
Percival David Foundation. See page 56

68. *Mallet-shaped vase with fish handles. Lung-ch'üan ware (Kinuta type). Sung dynasty. Ht. 9 in. Baron Iwasaki. See page 56*

69. *Incense burner with stylized fish handles. Lung-ch'üan ware
(Kinuta type). Sung dynasty. Diam. (with handles)* 7·3 *in.
Percival David Foundation. See page* 56

70. *Vase or beaker. Lung-ch'üan ware. Sung dynasty. Ht. 7·2 in.*
Nezu Museum, Tokyo. See page 56

71. *Vase in the form of a jade ritual vessel.*
Lung-ch'üan ware (Kinuta type). Sung dynasty. Ht. c. 14 in.
Japanese collection. See page 57

72. *Vase of bronze form with fish handles.*
Lung ch'üan ware (Kinuta type). Sung dynasty.
Japanese collection. See pages 56, 57

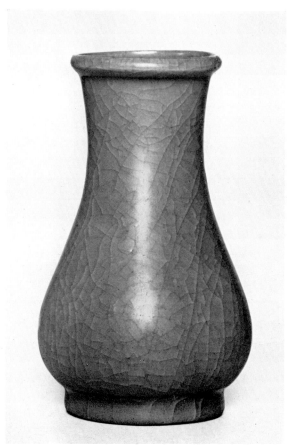

73A. *Foliate cup. Lung-ch'üan ware (Kinuta type). Sung dynasty.*
Diam. 3¾ *in. See page* 56
73B. *Vase with heavily crazed glaze. Lung-ch'üan ware. Sung dynasty.*
Ht. 5⅞ *in.*
Mrs. Alfred Clark. See page 56

74A. *Bowl with moulded lotus-petal design outside. Lung-ch'üan ware (Kinuta type). Sung dynasty. Diam. 6½ in. See page 56*
74B. *Shallow dish with moulded lotus-petal design outside. Lung-ch'üan ware (Kinuta type). Sung dynasty. Diam. 6½ in.*
City Art Gallery, Bristol. See page 56

75. *Small dish with incised decoration of fish. Lung-ch'üan ware (Kinuta type). Sung dynasty. Diam. 5$\frac{1}{8}$ in. City Art Gallery, Bristol. See page* 56

76. *Vase of spotted celadon ('tobi seiji'). Lung-ch'üan ware.
Late Sung or Yüan. Ht. 10·8 in.
Mr. Konoike. See page 57*

77. *Dish with dragon decoration in relief. Lung-ch'üan ware.*
Late Sung or Yüan.
Japanese collection. See page 56

78. *Covered vase with horizontal ribbing. Chekiang celadon.*
Late Sung or Yüan. Ht. 8¾ in.
Museum of Eastern Art, Oxford (Ingram Collection). See page 55

79A. *Small conical bowl with carved decoration of flowering prunus spray under a light green glaze. Chekiang celadon.*
Late Sung or Yüan. Diam. 5 in.
Rijksmuseum, Amsterdam. See page 55
79B. *Dish with two dragons in biscuit relief. Lung-ch'üan ware.*
Late Sung or Yüan. Diam. c. 7 in.
Japanese collection. See page 57

80A. *Ritual vessel with floral decoration in relief. Lung-ch'üan ware.*
Late Sung or Yüan. See page 56

80B. *Barrel-shaped vessel with floral decoration in relief. Lung-ch'üan ware.*
Late Sung or Yüan.
Japanese collection. See page 56

81. *Pear-shaped vase with carved lotus scrolls*
above overlapping lotus-petals. Lung-ch'üan ware (Tenryūji type).
Yüan dynasty. Ht. $9\frac{5}{16}$ *in.*
Mrs. Alfred Clark. See page 61

82. *Vase with flaring mouth and decoration of peony scrolls in relief;*
under the lip an incised inscription dated 4th year of the T'ai Ting
period (1327). Lung-ch'üan ware (Tenryūji type).
Yüan dynasty. Ht. 28 in.
Percival David Foundation. See page 61

83. *Basin with dragon, cloud scrolls and flowers in biscuit relief.*
Lung-ch'üan ware. Yüan dynasty. Diam. 16·95 in.
Percival David Foundation. See pages 57, 62

84. *Ewer. Lung-ch'üan ware. Yüan dynasty. Ht. 9·4 in.*
Percival David Foundation. See page 61

85A. *Vase of spotted celadon ('tobi seiji'). Lung-ch'üan ware.*
Yüan or early Ming. See page 57
85B. *Peach-shaped cup with leaves in relief. Lung-ch'üan ware.*
Yüan or early Ming.
Japanese collection. See page 61

86. *Square flask with dragon and cloud scrolls in relief within quatrefoil
panel; loop handles on the top and sides. Lung-ch'üan ware.
Yüan or early Ming. Diam. 13·8 in.
Percival David Foundation. See page 62*

87. *Pear-shaped vase with long slender neck and tubular handles,
the body decorated with carved peonies under a pale green glaze.
Chekiang celadon. Early Ming. Ht. 8¾ in.
Sir Alan Barlow. See page 61*

88. *Vase with flaring mouth (cut down at the lip) and incised decoration of floral scrolls; on the neck an inscribed panel dated 7th year of Hsüan Tê period (1432). Lung-ch'üan ware (Tenryūji type). Ming dynasty. Ht. 17·3 in. Percival David Foundation. See page 61*

89. *Basin with moulded* tou-niu *pursuing a sacred pearl.*
Lung-ch'üan ware. Probably early Ming. Diam. 14 *in.*
City Art Gallery, Bristol. See page 63

90. *Vase with flaring mouth and incised decoration of lotus scrolls;
on the neck an inscribed panel dated 5th year of the Ching T'ai period
(1454). Lung-ch'üan ware (Tenryūji type).
Ming dynasty. Ht. 26·8 in.
Percival David Foundation. See page 61*

91. *Large bowl incised with peony, lotus-petal and thunder patterns; an
elaborate lotus-blossom medallion stamped in relief in the centre and
radial fluting inside; a recessed circular hole in the base.
Lung-ch'üan ware. Ming dynasty. Diam. 16½ in.
Percival David Foundation. See page 61*

92. *Large dish with incised decoration of dragon among cloud scrolls and floral arabesques round the sides. Lung-ch'üan ware. Ming dynasty. Diam. 16½ in. Percival David Foundation. See page* 61

93A. *Vase with moulded and incised floral decoration.*
Lung-ch'üan ware (Shichikan type). Ming dynasty.
Japanese collection. See page 64
93B. *Flower-pot on three legs with inscription incised under the glaze,*
recording that ten vessels were made for a resident of Li-shui hsien in
Ch'u-chou prefecture in the year 1517. *Ch'u-chou ware.*
Ming dynasty. Diam. 8·8 *in.*
Percival David Foundation. See page 64

94. *Vase (mei-p'ing) lightly carved with dragon design under a pale celadon glaze. Ching-tê-chên ware. Ch'ing dynasty (K'ang Hsi mark and period). Ht. 7⅜ in. Museum of Eastern Art, Oxford. See page 66*

95A. *Stem-cup with pale green glaze. Ching-tê-chên ware.*
Ch'ing dynasty (Yung Chêng period). Ht. 3·9 in.
Fitzwilliam Museum, Cambridge. See page 66
95B. *Shallow bowl with crackled blue-green glaze. Ching-tê-chên ware*
(Kuan type). Ch'ing dynasty. Diam. 7 in.
City Art Gallery, Bristol. See page 67

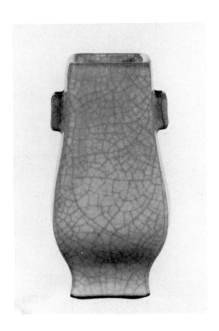

96A. *Small vase with crackled blue-green glaze. Ching-tê-chên ware (Kuan type). Ch'ing dynasty (Yung Chêng mark and period). Ht. 3·4 in. See page 67*

96B. *Bowl lightly carved outside with flowers and leaves under a pale celadon glaze; inside is the character* ying *('tomb') in underglaze blue. Ching-tê-chên ware. Ch'ing dynasty (K'ang Hsi mark and period). Diam. 6·1 in. Museum of Fine Arts, Boston (Hoyt Collection). See page 66*